I Am America

WHEN THE EARTH DRAGON TREMBLED

A Story of Chinatown During the
San Francisco Earthquake and Fire

Book design by Jake Slavik
Illustrations by Eric Freeberg

Photographs ©: Library of Congress, 148 (top), 148 (bottom), 149 (top), 149 (bottom), 150

Published in the United States by Jolly Fish Press, an imprint of North Star Editions, Inc.

First Edition
First Printing, 2020

This is a work of fiction. Names, characters, places, and incidents are either the product of the author's imagination or are used fictitiously, and any resemblance to actual persons living or dead, business establishments, events, or locales is entirely coincidental.

Library of Congress Cataloging-in-Publication Data
Names: Cummings, Judy Dodge, author. | Freeberg, Eric, illustrator.
Title: When the earth dragon trembled : a story of Chinatown during the San
    Francisco earthquake and fire / by Judy Dodge Cummings ; illustrated by
    Eric Freeberg.
Description: First edition. | Mendota Heights, Minnesota : Jolly Fish
    Press, [2021] | Series: I am America | Summary: Han Liu rejects his
    father's attempts to teach him traditional Chinese values, but when an
    earthquake and fire strike Chinatown, separating Han from his father, a
    book of family proverbs is all Han has left to guide him. Includes
    author's note.
Identifiers: LCCN 2020001272 (print) | LCCN 2020001273 (ebook) | ISBN
    9781631634901 (hardcover) | ISBN 9781631634918 (paperback) | ISBN
    9781631634925 (ebook)
Subjects: CYAC: Fathers and sons–Fiction. | Manners and customs–Fiction.
    | Chinatown (San Francisco, Calif.)–Fiction. | San Francisco
    (Calif.)–History–20th century–Fiction. | San Francisco Earthquake and
    Fire, Calif., 1906–Fiction.
Classification: LCC PZ7.1.C855 Wh 2021 (print) | LCC PZ7.1.C855 (ebook) |
    DDC [Fic]–dc23
LC record available at https://lccn.loc.gov/2020001272
LC ebook record available at https://lccn.loc.gov/2020001273

Jolly Fish Press
North Star Editions, Inc.
2297 Waters Drive
Mendota Heights, MN 55120
www.jollyfishpress.com

Printed in the United States of America

I Am America

WHEN THE EARTH DRAGON TREMBLED

♦

A Story of Chinatown During the San Francisco Earthquake and Fire

By Judy Dodge Cummings

Illustrated by Eric Freeberg

Consultant: Lei Qin, PhD, Assistant Adjunct Professor of Modern
Chinese Culture and History, University of California, Los Angeles

JOLLY
FiSH
PRESS

Mendota Heights, Minnesota

Chapter 1

April 17, 1906 — 4:30 p.m.

$\mathcal{T}$he box of groceries nagged Han from its perch on the counter. He was to deliver it to a house outside of Chinatown. *Not just yet.* An off-key hum drifted from the storeroom, where Father was counting inventory. Through the shop's front window, Han watched a man and two little boys cross the street. Each boy's long braid swung from side to side, as if the queues danced to a rhythm only they could hear.

Han crossed his fingers and waited. The trio passed by. He had the store to himself and enough time for some adventure.

Plunging his hand into a jar of sugared almonds, Han grabbed one and popped it into his mouth. He crunched down on the treat and picked up the novel Miss Cameron had loaned him for the third time this year. He opened the book to his favorite scene: a murder in a graveyard at midnight.

As Han read, his mind entered the story and the room around him transformed. Store shelves became the branches of an elm tree. Barrels of dried oysters, abalone, and cuttlefish turned into tombstones. The Chinese lantern that dangled from the ceiling was the full moon.

Han turned the page. Three men stood beside an open grave. One was a doctor who wanted to experiment on the corpse in the coffin. The other two were outcasts hired to dig up the body. The diggers demanded more money, but the doctor refused.

A thrill of excitement crept up Han's spine as the diggers and doctor grappled.

Han's heart beat faster as one digger picked up a knife.

The man lunged for the doctor.

The knife hovered above the doctor's chest.

Suddenly, the book disappeared from Han's hand.

He looked up and blinked.

The graveyard had vanished. Han was back behind the counter of the Liu Grocery & Dry Goods store on the corner of Dupont and Clay Streets in Chinatown, San Francisco. Next to him stood Father, an angry scowl on his face and *The Adventures of Tom Sawyer* in his hand.

"Why are you still here?" Father nodded at the box on the counter. "The Zhangs are waiting for their groceries."

Guilt and irritation battled in Han's stomach. Guilt won.

"Sorry, Father," he said. "I just sold some sugared almonds to Miss Cameron, and she loaned me this book. I'll make the delivery now."

Father's scowl deepened, turning his eyebrows into a furry brown caterpillar. "Miss Cameron? The white woman who runs the Occidental Mission Home for Girls?"

Han nodded.

Father glared at the open jar of nuts on the counter. "That woman feeds those wayward girls too many sweets."

Han screwed on the lid and returned the jar to the shelf. "But she pays for them, so it's good for business." He eyed the book Father held. "May I have that back?"

Father fanned the pages of *Tom Sawyer*, stopping now and then to study an illustration. His lip curled up as though the book stank.

Setting the novel down on the counter a little too hard, Father asked, "Why aren't you reading *Three Character Classic* for your Chinese class?"

"I already memorized my couplets for tonight," Han said.

Father's big fingers drummed on the cover of *Tom Sawyer*. "Well then, if you have extra time to read, don't waste it on this American nonsense." Tucking the novel under his arm, Father walked across the shop floor. He disappeared down the hallway that led into the back bedroom.

"That book belongs to Miss Cameron!" Han called after him.

A few seconds later, Father returned. Instead of *Tom Sawyer*, he now held a small paperback. Father carefully set the tired-looking book on the counter and pushed it slowly toward Han.

"Your grandfather's grandfather compiled this book of Chinese proverbs almost one hundred years ago." His voice had turned gentle. "My father gave it to me when I was eighteen, right after we arrived in San Francisco. He knew living in a strange land would be hard and that I'd need something to guide me."

Father smoothed the cover of the book as if it were a favorite pet or a beloved child's cheek. Except Han did not ever recall Father stroking his cheek so tenderly.

"You are only twelve years old, Han, but your mother is not here to guide you, and I'm busy with all this." Father spread his arms wide. His broad chest and muscular arms practically blocked the light coming through the windows.

"The time has come for you to take possession of this collection of family wisdom." He patted the book. "The sayings in here will teach you more than Tom Sawyer ever could. Memorize these proverbs. They'll serve you in troubled times."

Han eyed the book. The cover must have once been red, but had since faded to the color of rotten salmon. *Proverbs* was written in gold Chinese characters across the front. He slid the book back to Father. "You keep it. It's old and fragile. I wouldn't want to damage it."

Han hopped down from the stool and picked up the box of groceries. "Besides, I'm busy too. Helping out with the store." Han balanced the box on one hip. "And at regular school every day, I have to memorize multiplication tables and boring English grammar."

Father clicked his tongue.

"Then I have to memorize couplets for Chinese school every night," Han continued. "I can't expect my brain to remember proverbs too."

Another tongue click, louder this time.

A slow burn started in Han's stomach. "Besides, I like *The Adventures of Tom Sawyer*. It's exciting. And funny." He pointed at *Proverbs*. "I bet that's not a bit funny."

"Intelligence is endowed, but wisdom is earned," Father said.

Han rolled his eyes. When Mother and Meiying had taken Grandfather's body back to China last year for a proper burial, Father's sense of fun had disappeared over the horizon with their ship. He clung to Chinese traditions like they were a life raft and he was drowning.

Father saw Han's eye roll. His light-brown face flushed, and he went to the table by the woodstove and picked up a pencil and notebook. Returning to the counter, Father set both items beside the book of proverbs.

"There will be plenty of time to memorize some proverbs now that you won't be reading Mr. Sawyer." Father's voice was hard. "After you deliver that box to the Zhangs, you will go to Chinese school. Then tonight you will choose one proverb from this book. You will memorize it, write down an explanation of what it means, and then show me your work. You will do this every day with a new proverb."

Han bit his tongue so he wouldn't say something to make the punishment worse.

"This is important." Some of the anger leaked out of Father's voice. "America is a confusing country. Once we've saved enough money to buy property in China, you and I will return and be reunited with your mother and sister. You must keep the Chinese ways until we find our way home again."

America is my home. Han thought these words, but dared not say them. Instead, he spoke around the idea. "Why don't we just bring Mother and Meiying back here?"

Father smacked his palm against the yellowed copy of the English-language newspaper that had been pinned to the wall for years.

May 7, 1902
San Francisco Call

EDITORIAL: THREAT OF YELLOW PERIL IS OVER

Twenty years ago, Congress passed the Chinese Exclusion Act. This law banned Chinese laborers from immigrating to the United States for ten years and prevented Chinese people from becoming naturalized American citizens.

The law was needed because the Chinese working in the mines and on the railroads were willing to work for starvation wages. This "Yellow Peril" stole jobs from red-blooded American men.

In 1892, the Exclusion Act was renewed for ten more years, and now Congress has made the ban on Chinese immigration permanent. Any Chinese person who leaves the United States will not be allowed to reenter unless they meet strict qualifications.

Soon, California will once again be a land of white people only. The way it was meant to be.

"This is why!" Father bit the words out and spit them at Han. "The government has locked Chinese people out!"

Han shifted the box of groceries back onto the counter with a thud. "But if you hadn't forced Mother to take Grandfather's bones back to China in the first place, she and Meiying wouldn't be stuck there!" Han yelled.

Father grabbed *Proverbs* off the counter and flipped through it. When he found what he was looking for, he stabbed a sentence with an accusing finger. "'If we have none to foul the bed, we shall have none to burn the paper at our grave!'"

Han raised his hands. "'Foul the bed?' What does that mean?"

"That means," Father snapped, "if a husband and wife have no children, then there is no one to carry out the proper rituals when they die. If the proper rituals are not observed, the spirits of the dead grow restless and angry." Father pointed at Han. "It is the son's responsibility to care for his parents—even after they die. Especially after they die."

"You were Grandfather's son, so why did you make Mother take his body to China?"

Father sighed heavily. "How could I leave your mother, a woman, alone in a foreign land to run the store?" He set *Proverbs* down in front of Han. "Clearly, you don't know what it means to be Chinese. You need this book."

Han dared not push Father any more, but he had to know one thing. "When can I get *Tom Sawyer* back?"

Father stared at Han for a long moment. Then he returned to the storeroom without another word.

Han's fingers twitched. He wanted to fling *Proverbs* across the room. Instead, he flicked the cover with his thumb and forefinger. Then he picked up the box of groceries and stomped out of the store, letting the door slam shut behind him. It was risky for a Chinese boy to go outside the borders of Chinatown alone, but right now Han was glad the Zhang house was several blocks away. He wanted to escape Father and all his old ways.

Chapter 2

April 17, 1906 — 5:15 p.m.

*M*ason Street was noisy. Cable cars rattled by. Automobiles growled as drivers zigged and zagged around pedestrians. Newspaper boys cried out the evening headlines, and horses clopped past with wagons in tow. But Han did not hear a thing. His mind kept replaying what he had seen inside the Zhangs' house.

When he had arrived with the groceries, Rose Zhang had opened the door. She was in Han's sixth-grade class at public school. As Han followed her down a wide, paneled hallway to the kitchen, they passed an open door. Han glanced inside. What he saw made him stop and stare, his mouth open in astonishment.

Overflowing bookshelves lined the walls from floor to ceiling. "You have so many books!" Han said.

"That's my papa's study," Rose said.

Han looked at her. "Has your father read all these?"

She shrugged. "Probably. Some are Mama's, and the books on the bottom shelf belong to me and my brothers."

Han leaned into the doorway, squinting at the lower shelf. There were at least twenty-five books there. One title caught his eye. *The Adventures of Tom Sawyer*. "These books are in English."

Rose gave him a funny look. "Of course. We're Americans."

A hot flush climbed up Han's neck. As he trailed Rose to the kitchen, he glanced down at his wide-legged pants and long tunic. Did Rose think he wasn't an American because he dressed like a Chinese boy?

A shout snapped Han back to the present. He was standing on the curb of California Street, about to step into the path of an oncoming buckboard loaded with sacks of grain. The wagon driver glared at him. "Watch yourself, boy."

Han stepped back and waited until the buckboard had passed before darting across the street. Then he realized his mistake. He should have taken a different route home.

Halfway up the block was the Fairmont Hotel. The brand-new building was scheduled to open in two weeks. Made of gray granite and standing seven stories high, the Fairmont looked like a palace from its perch atop Nob Hill. But it was not the hotel that caused Han's chest to tighten. It was the boys in front of the building.

Two white boys. They looked roughly Han's age. One kid was stocky, and his head rested directly on his shoulders as if it had no use for a neck. The taller boy had ears the size of an elephant's.

"Hey," said Elephant Ears. "Do you wanna buy some Wrigley's?" He held up a carton, its lid open to reveal packs of spearmint gum.

Han tugged his hat down to make sure his queue was still tucked snugly inside. He plastered on a fake smile. "No, thank you."

The boy without a neck stepped in front of him. "Why not? It's only a nickel."

"I don't have a nickel," Han said.

"Oh, come on," said Elephant Ears. "You got a nickel."

"No nickel." Han lifted up his long tunic and pulled out both pockets of his pants to show they were empty. "No money."

Han stepped to the right.

No-neck stepped right too, staring at Han with unblinking green eyes.

"No nickee," said Elephant Ears in a singsong voice. "No money."

Han stepped to the left. No-neck moved left too.

"Tell the truth," said Elephant Ears. "You just don't like gum, do you?"

Han lunged to the right, but No-neck was fast. He blocked Han again and stepped closer. Han's nostrils tingled at the piney scent of spearmint on the boy's breath.

"You don't like gum because you're Chinese," Elephant Ears said, "and the only thing Chinese people like to eat is rat meat. Ain't that right?"

"Or cat meat," said No-neck.

Han had had enough. He shoved No-neck in the chest, but the boy was built like a boulder and he barely budged.

"You wanna fight, China?" No-neck whacked Han on the side of his head. The blow sent Han's hat flying. His queue sprang free and slithered down his back.

Before Han could run, Elephant Ears grabbed the end of the braid.

"Let go of me!" Han yelled.

Elephant Ears yanked hard. Han lost his balance and fell to the ground, his right hip landing on the cobblestones. It felt like his queue was being pulled out by the roots as Elephant Ears dragged him into an alley. Han shuffled backward like a crab to reduce the pressure on his braid, his hands scraping against gravel and rocks and something slimy.

The late afternoon sunlight barely reached inside the narrow alley. No-neck stood in front of Han, his face cast in shadow. "People like you don't belong here," he said. "People who eat rats and cats."

Han kicked out one leg, but No-neck jumped out of his way. "I don't eat rats or cats!" Han shouted. "Let me go!"

"Giddyup!" Elephant Ears whipped Han's queue up and down. Han's scalp felt like it was on fire.

"Come on, horsey," Elephant Ears said. "Maybe there are some tasty rats in here." He dragged Han toward a pile of chicken bones and apple cores. Flies buzzed around the smelly heap.

Han gripped his braid with both hands and leaned forward. Elephant Ears pulled in the opposite direction.

No-neck smacked his leg and laughed. "It's a hairy tug-of-war!"

A shadow darkened the alley entrance. Through eyes blurry with pain, Han saw a familiar figure enter the lane. It was Lung Tin, the Chinese peddler who lived a few blocks from Han. The skinny old man carried a wooden pole over his shoulders, a basket of fruit hanging from each end. Han opened his mouth to warn Lung Tin to run. The peddler was as thin as a whittled broom handle and no match for these bullies.

But before Han could say a word, Lung Tin slid the baskets off the pole and swung the long stick at No-neck's backside.

The boy howled. Gripping his rear end with both hands, he whipped around. "Get out of here, old man!" No-neck took a threatening step forward.

Lung Tin shoved the boy in the belly with one end of the pole, pinning him against the alley wall. No-neck howled again, but did not struggle with the pole pressed against his gut.

"Let him loose!" yelled Elephant Ears. "Or I'll pull this kid's hair out."

Elephant Ears yanked on the braid and a shrill cry of pain escaped Han's lips. Lung Tin pivoted. Swinging the pole, he brought it down on Elephant Ears's wrist.

Han's braid was suddenly free, and he fell back in relief on the cobblestones.

Elephant Ears cradled his wrist to his chest. "Dirty, rotten rat-eaters!" he yelled.

Han scrambled to his knees to prepare for a fight, but the boy just swore at him before running out the back end of the alley with No-neck hot on his heels.

Han massaged his head, trying to rub away the burning pain. "Thank you, Lung Tin. It was two against one, and I was in trouble."

The man regarded Han, his face as brown and rutted as a dried riverbed. "Are you hurt?"

Han turned his hands over. Both palms were scratched. His left ear stung where No-neck had smacked him, and his right side throbbed. Han raised his tunic. A bruise the size and color of an eggplant had already formed above his hip. But at least he still had his scalp.

"I'm okay," he said.

Lung Tin refastened the fruit baskets to the ends of his pole. "The same thing used to happen to me whenever I stepped foot outside Chinatown." His voice crackled with age and experience. "That's why I cut off my queue. Years ago."

Han squinted at the peddler's black cap. He had assumed Lung Tin wore his queue wound around his head under his cap, the way Father did.

"But Chinese law says all males must wear the queue," Han said.

Lung Tin nodded. "Chinese law says that, but I live in America."

"Don't you want to return to China?" Han thought that everyone born in China wanted to go back some day. Father sure did.

Lung Tin shrugged. "I'd like to, of course. But if I don't survive in America, I'll never get back to China, and the queue was making it hard for me to survive." He patted Han's braid. "It's too easy for our enemies to grab."

Han put a protective hand to his head and smiled weakly. "I know."

Han grabbed his hat, then he and Lung Tin exited the alley and walked north on Mason Street. The adrenaline from the fight still pumped through Han's veins.

"I never want to move to China." Han looked up at Lung Tin to gauge his reaction. He had not dared admit this to Father. "I'm an American."

The peddler jerked his head back in the direction of the Fairmont. "Those white boys don't think you are."

"Those white boys are stupid," Han muttered. "I'm as American as they are."

"Well then," Lung Tin said, "why do you still have that attached to your head?" He nodded at Han's braid.

Han did not reply, because he had no good answer.

When they reached Clay Street, Han bade Lung Tin goodbye and turned right while the peddler turned left. As he walked home, Han took a hard look at his neighborhood. Gambling houses lined the street, eighteen on one block alone. Gold, pearl, and jade ornaments glittered in the windows of jewelry stores. The signs on Chinese souvenir shops were painted gaudy red and gold to lure in white tourists. The thud of hammers drifted out of a storefront shoe factory.

The smells of Chinatown were so familiar that Han did not notice them unless he paid attention. The iron scent of blood came from a meat shop where the butcher hacked apart a pig carcass. Freshly killed chickens hung from the shop's ceiling, and live fowl clucked nervously in crates on the floor. The salty stench of fish blew down from rooftops where fishmongers dried their catch in the sun. Produce stands sent the sweet scent of fresh berries and citrus to passersby. Here and there, the pungent odor of horse manure wafted up from the cobblestone streets. The door to a basement-level restaurant stood open, and Han's mouth watered at the aroma of roasted pork with garlic and ginger.

Everywhere there were people. Men strolled in and out of gambling houses. A toothless old woman haggled with a man selling cabbages. A mother and little boy emerged from a tailor's shop. A thin girl stood in a doorway, staring listlessly at Han as he walked past. Old men played mahjong on the sidewalk outside a general store. Chinatown was crowded, but to Han it felt cozy, safe, and familiar.

When he reached the Liu Grocery & Dry Goods store, Han stood on the sidewalk and studied the building his grandfather and father had bought back in 1884. The shop windows were smudged, and there was a small tear in the green awning that shaded the sidewalk. But the red sign with its black letters painted in both English and Chinese looked bold and proud.

San Francisco was home. Han did not want to move to China. He did not want to leave the country of his birth. But he also did not want white boys to rip out his hair whenever he stepped outside Chinatown.

Han thought about what Lung Tin had said and knew what he had to do. He also knew that Father would not like it. Inhaling deeply to steel his nerves, Han opened the shop door and walked inside.

Chapter 3

April 17, 1906 — 6:00 p.m.

A burst of laughter and a cloud of cigar smoke greeted Han as he entered the store. With a sinking heart, he realized it was game night.

Father sat at the table, a fat cigar in his hand. Around him were Mr. Yep, the fishmonger from next door; Mr. Sing, the herbalist who operated the apothecary across the street; and Mr. Lock, the barber who owned a shop on Waverly Street. The ebony mahjong box sat at Father's feet, and game tiles lay facedown on the table. A grin split Father's face from ear to ear.

"Han, we're glad you're home," Mr. Sing called. "Take your father's place. He wins too much."

Before Han could make a polite excuse, Father spoke for him. "Han has work to do." He caught Han's eye and looked meaningfully at the book of proverbs and the notebook that still sat on the counter.

Han lifted his chin. Father treated him like a child. Any last inkling of doubt he had about what he intended to do vanished.

"My father is right," Han said as he picked up the books. "I have work to do. I hope your luck improves, Mr. Sing."

Han retreated down the hallway to the back room he and Father shared. Before Grandfather died, the family had rented a small apartment from the white landlord who owned the building next door. But when Mother and Meiying returned to China with Grandfather's bones, Father and Han did not need so much space. Now Han wished he had more privacy.

Two iron bed frames stood side by side. Han ran his hand over the red, yellow, and blue quilt that covered his bed. Mother had made this blanket for him. He wished she were here now. Mother would not like what Han was about to do, but she would understand why he had to do it, and she would explain to Father.

Han set *Proverbs* and the notebook on Father's bed and knelt on the floor. Reaching under the bed, he pushed aside the chamber pot and pulled out a basket Mother had left behind. He found her sewing shears and took them to the mirror that hung above the bureau.

Considering his reflection, Han wondered what those white boys had seen that made them target him. His skin was light brown, while their flesh was the color of seagull droppings and looked just as pasty.

What about his eyes? Han leaned closer to the mirror and widened them. Mother said his eyes would win a girl's heart someday. Maybe No-neck's mother loved her son's eyes too, but Han doubted they would win a girl's heart. No-neck had eyes the color of dried seaweed.

The long braid that draped across Han's shoulder like a rat's tail drew his gaze. Lung Tin was right. It was Han's queue that made him vulnerable. In America, braids were for girls. Not boys.

In one swift move, Han picked up the shears, reached behind his head, and snipped off his braid. It fell to the floor with a soft plop. The skin on the back of Han's neck felt cool and dangerously naked. He exhaled a long, shaky breath. The first step of his plan was done. Now for step two.

Han picked up *Proverbs*, paging through it to find a saying to match his mood. His eyes fell on one line. Energy buzzed through Han's body as he wrote his interpretation. He felt light, almost giddy, but the pencil marks on the page were dark, angry, and determined.

Han's heart galloped like a racehorse in his chest. Now it was time for step three, the hardest of all. He picked the queue up off the floor and slipped it into his pocket. With the notebook and *Proverbs* in hand, Han walked back down the hallway. But Father's friends were still in the store, and this conversation needed to be private.

He waited in the hallway where he could not be seen, hoping the men would leave before his courage disappeared.

"Did you hear the rumors about that Reinbach fellow?" Mr. Lock asked.

"Jacob Reinbach?" Father asked. "The owner of the cigar factory on Sacramento Street?"

"Yes, that Reinbach," Mr. Lock said.

Han ran a hand up the back of his neck. With each passing second, he felt his courage retreating. Little spiders of anxiety were taking its place.

Proverb: "Having something to say,
speak plainly, never conceal it."

Interpretation: If you have something important
to tell someone, don't be afraid to speak up.

Father,

I do have something to say, so I will speak plainly.
Speaking Chinese, dressing Chinese, and acting
Chinese make me different from other American
boys. I don't want to be different.

No more Chinese school in the evening.
No more queue.
No more interpreting Chinese proverbs.
I am an American.

"What I heard—" Mr. Lock continued.

Han groaned silently and leaned his head against the hallway wall. Sometimes Mr. Lock's stories lasted ages.

"—is that he hides his money in his icebox."

For what felt like hours, but was probably only five minutes, Han listened to Mr. Lock's story about Jacob Reinbach. The white businessman had lost all his bank savings in the financial panic of 1896, so now he converted all his cash into gold bars and stored them in his icebox.

Finally, chairs scraped on the wooden floor, and the men said their goodbyes. Han heard the shop door bang shut behind them. To call back his courage, he squeezed his eyes closed and remembered the dark alley.

No-neck's hot breath in his face. Elephant Ears shouting, "Giddyup!" The stink of garbage mingled with the sharp scent of Han's fear.

The memory of that humiliation bolstered his courage, and he walked into the store. Father stood behind the counter, the ledger in front of him. Han set *Proverbs* and the notebook beside the ledger.

"I want *The Adventures of Tom Sawyer*." The words flew out, and Han wanted to snatch them back. He had not meant to start this way.

Father looked up, one bushy eyebrow raised. "Aren't you hungry?" He gestured at the stove, where the large copper wok held rice and meat.

"No."

Father bent over the ledger again. "Don't you need to leave for Chinese school?"

"No," Han repeated.

"Why not?"

Han pushed out the words quickly. "I don't need to leave for Chinese school because I'm quitting Chinese school."

Father raised his head slowly. "What?"

"I'm quitting Chinese school." Han's voice cracked on the words.

Father's mouth hardened into a narrow line. "It's closing time. Please lock the door."

Han turned, exposing his newly hairless neck. Tension vibrated in the air as he walked to the door. He slid the bolt. The click sounded like a gunshot, and Han flinched.

When he turned around, Father's eyes pinned him in place. "What have you done?" Father growled.

"I will no longer wear the queue." Han hated the quiver in his voice.

"You disrespect me so much?"

"My hair has nothing to do with you, Father," Han said.

Father let out an exasperated sigh. "It has everything to do with me. The lifespan of the father of a boy who cuts off his queue is shortened. I will die young because of your selfishness."

Han waved this away. "That's just a story, Father. It's the twentieth century. Nobody believes that anymore." He dropped into a chair by the table, suddenly exhausted.

"Do you believe in the law?" Father slammed the ledger shut. "Because the law in China requires all men and teenage boys to wear the queue." He pointed at Han.

"You'll be locked up the minute you step off the boat. How will your mother feel about that?"

Han shook his head. "That won't happen, because I'll never move to China."

Father drew back. "You never want to see your mother and sister again?"

Clenching his fists, Han struggled not to lose his temper. "Of course I want to see them. But I don't want to live in China." A lump rose in his throat. Father was not being fair. "It's your fault anyway."

A snort of laughter erupted from Father. "My fault? My fault that you cut your queue? My fault that you whine like a spoiled American child?"

Han jumped to his feet, sending the chair screeching back in protest. "It's your fault that Mother and Meiying are stuck in China. You sent them."

Father slammed his fist on the counter. "I am ashamed to have such a disobedient son! I am ashamed to have a son with no respect for Chinese ways! I'm ashamed to have a son who threatens our family's future."

"What about what threatens me?" Han shouted. He marched to the counter. Yanking up his tunic, he turned to expose the ugly bruise that fanned his right hip. "This is what Chinese ways got me today when two white boys decided to drag me by my queue into a dark alley."

Father stared at Han's hip. His mouth hung open, but no words came out. Emotion flickered beneath the anger in Father's expression. Was it regret or shame or disappointment? Han could not tell. Pulling the queue out of his pocket, Han tossed it on the counter. Then he opened the notebook.

"I interpreted a proverb. Just like you asked." He handed the notebook to Father.

As he read, Father's jaw hardened, and Han geared up for another explosion. Instead, Father closed the notebook and set it on top of *Proverbs*. He picked up the queue, cradled it in his palm, and slowly stroked it. Han shifted from foot to foot in the deafening silence.

When Father finally spoke, his voice was quiet but heavy. "Xiào gǎndòng tiān."

Han blinked rapidly. "I don't understand."

Father rested one heavy hand on Han's shoulder and spoke slowly and clearly in English. "I said that Confucius teaches us that filial piety moves heaven and earth."

"I know what the words are," Han said, shrugging off Father's touch. "I just don't understand what it means."

"It means that when a son shows proper respect and obedience to his parents, this filial piety protects the universe from disorder and chaos."

"I wasn't trying to be disrespectful, Father," Han interrupted.

"But when a child dishonors his parent," Father went on, "the universe is tipped out of balance."

It took all Han's willpower not to groan. More superstition. "Are you going to punish me?" He might as well hear his sentence now instead of worrying all night.

Bending his head over the ledger again, Father said, "Oh, you will be punished, my son. You should hope it comes from me and not from a power far greater."

Han frowned. "You mean like the Chinese emperor?"

"I mean fate," Father said.

That night, the windowless bedroom was dark and the April night cool, but Han could not sleep. Father's mysterious words made him uneasy. Punching his pillow, Han told himself to forget about what Father said. Fate was just another word for superstition.

Chapter 4

April 18, 1906 — 5:12 a.m.

$\mathcal{T}$he mountainous waves blocked Han's view of China. Determined to drown him, the sea tossed the ship from side to side. Han clung to the railing, but it was useless. The storm roared like an angry beast, and Han knew he should have stayed in America.

"Xing xing!" Father's voice penetrated the roar. "Wake up!"

Han opened his eyes, expecting to see a giant wave bearing down on him. Instead, he saw Father's desk. It was moving. The desk leaped forward and then zigzagged to the right. Han realized his body was moving too.

Up and down.

Side to side.

Was Han still in the middle of a nightmare?

"What's happening?" he cried.

"Dey loong jun!" Father yelled from his bed. "The Earth Dragon has awakened!"

Han gripped the side of his bed and pulled himself upright. Di zhen le! It was an earthquake! A second later, a chunk of plaster fell from the ceiling, landing where his head had just been. A cloud of dust enveloped him.

The shelf on the wall snapped, sending Father's small book collection crashing to the floor. Through eyes filled with grit, Han saw the cover of *The Adventures of Tom Sawyer*. He had to save Miss Cameron's book. Sliding off the bed, Han tried to walk. The floor bucked and heaved like an angry horse. He dropped to all fours and crawled toward the book.

"We must get out of here!" Father shouted.

Another chunk of ceiling crashed down behind Han, and he abandoned *Tom Sawyer*. As fast as he could, Han crawled down the hall, Father right behind him. The only door to the street was through the store.

With one last tremor, the ground stopped shaking. Han gaped in horror at the store. The room looked like it had been attacked by an angry mob. Barrels were tipped over, their contents spilled across the floor. In a sea of pickled cabbage swam dried fish and oysters. Shards of broken jars stuck up like shark fins. Part of the collapsed ceiling made an island beside the stove.

Father gasped, and Han jerked around to see if he was hurt. But Father was staring straight ahead, through the shattered shop windows. Han followed his gaze and realized that things outside were even worse.

Dupont Street was humped and ridged. Electrical wires shot angry sparks from snapped poles. The walls of the Sings' apothecary had crumbled, but the frame still stood. On the second floor, Mrs. Sing sat up in bed, shrieking over and over. Part of Han wanted to tell her to be quiet and another part wanted to shriek along with her.

The earthquake had spit the fishmonger's stall into the middle of the street. Silvery fish carpeted the cobblestone street under a pile of broken boards and beams. Mr. Yep stood on the sidewalk, a dazed look on his face.

A body lay farther down the street. As Han recognized the face of the man, an arrow of pain pierced his heart. Lung Tin lay beside his wooden pole and baskets. Melons, peaches, and oranges rolled in the pool of blood flowing from under his head. Beside the peddler's cracked skull sat the murder weapon—the concrete cornice of the apothecary shop.

Bile rose in Han's throat.

"Come," Father said, rising to his feet. "Get dressed. We need to get outside." Han rose and followed Father back into their bedroom.

"But the earthquake is over," Han said as he slipped his shirt over his head. "Isn't it?"

"The dragon will tremble again," Father said. "It never trembles just once."

Father was right. They were barely outside before the earth began to shake again. Father shoved Han down to the ground and crouched over him. Even sheltered in the cocoon of Father's strong body, the terrified screams and crashing beams made the next twenty seconds seem like an eternity to Han.

When the earth finally stilled, the street was full of people, but everyone was strangely quiet. Mr. and Mrs. Sing stood nearby. Mrs. Sing wore a red nightgown. In one hand, she carried a birdcage that held four kittens, and a red-and-green parrot rode on her shoulder. Mr. Sing was dressed only in a nightshirt. He clutched his hands in front of his chest. Maybe he was praying, or maybe he was trying to make his hands stop shaking.

Han's mouth was full of grit. He tried to work up some spit while he watched Father crouch beside Lung Tin. Father removed a white handkerchief from his pocket and laid it over the dead man's face. A lump rose in Han's throat. Just yesterday the old man had rescued him.

"Are we safe now?" Han asked Father. "Will another quake strike?"

Father rose. The tendons in his thick neck stood out, his rapid pulse visible under the skin. His gaze flitted nervously in all directions. "The universe is out of balance." Father's voice was tinged with panic. "I told you last night this would happen. The imbalance has woken the Earth Dragon." He looked down at Lung Tin. "The Earth Dragon does not like to be disturbed."

Han touched the back of his neck where his queue should have been. Last night Father had told him filial piety kept the universe in balance. Han had cut off his braid, dropped out of Chinese school, and declared he would never move to China. He had known these actions would upset Father, yet he had done them anyway.

"But it was an earthquake," Han protested weakly. "Not a dragon. Dragons aren't real." Were they?

Father looked directly at Han then. "What else would tear the ground apart with such ferocity?" Fear flickered in his onyx-black eyes. Han had never seen Father afraid before, and the sight turned his blood to ice water. "We must pray the universe rights itself so the beast returns to its lair and does not embark upon a path of destruction aimed at those who woke it from its slumber."

Han felt as if a giant hand had reached inside his chest and plucked out his heart. He stared at the blood under Lung Tin's head. It had seeped between the cobblestones and was already the color of rust. Had he caused the peddler's death? Had his rejection of Chinese ways awoken the Earth Dragon? Would the beast come for him next?

SAN FRANCISCO DAILY NEWS

April 18, 1906

HUNDREDS DEAD!
DOWNTOWN FLATTENED.
CITY MAY BE DOOMED BECAUSE THERE IS NO WATER!

A massive earthquake struck San Francisco, California, at predawn today. The shock wave lasted over a minute and aftershocks buffeted the city for hours. At least 500 are dead. Many more are trapped in collapsed buildings. An estimated 50,000 people are homeless.

The Greek columns that ringed the dome of San Francisco City Hall toppled. Three of the four stories of the Valencia Hotel on Market Street sank into the marshy soil, drowning dozens. The Agnew Insane Asylum's central tower collapsed, crushing 117 patients.

The earthquake's shock waves overturned candles and heaters.

Stovepipes cracked and chimneys collapsed. As soon as the earth stopped shaking, the city ignited. Brave firefighters went into action. However, the quake ruptured hundreds of underground water pipes. When firefighters hooked hoses to hydrants, no water came out.

Fire Chief Dennis Sullivan might have had a solution, but he was severely injured in the earthquake and may not survive the night. The fate of San Francisco lies on the shoulders of Mayor Eugene Schmitz. Is he up to the task?

Only tomorrow will tell.

Chapter 5

April 18, 1906 — 9:00 a.m.

Portsmouth Square was packed. Most of Chinatown's residents were there and much of San Francisco's Italian population too. The plaza felt like the only safe place as small tremors continued to shake the ground. Men and women prayed out loud, and children wept. Han stayed very close to Father.

The sun smiled down at the city from a bright-blue sky. It was a cruel smile. How could the day be so beautiful above ground when underneath the Earth Dragon was trying to destroy them?

"Gōngniú!" shouted a man next to Han. He shoved Han aside and ran.

The crowd took up the cry. "Gōngniú!"

Han whirled around in confusion. A massive bull was charging toward him, its horns the size of elephant tusks. Han blinked. Was he dreaming again? How could a bull be in the middle of Portsmouth Square?

Father yanked Han by the arm, pulling him out of the animal's path. The bull veered to the right. People screamed and scattered.

A woman dressed in a nightgown picked up a rock and pelted the creature. "Huí qù dìxià!" she shouted.

In seconds, dozens of people echoed her cry. Stones bombarded the bull from all directions.

Han tugged Father's sleeve. "Why are they yelling at the bull to get back underground?"

A shot rang out, and Han jumped at the sound. The bull staggered, dropping to one knee. A police officer armed with a pistol approached the animal from behind and fired again into the animal's skull. It collapsed.

Han's heart galloped as quickly as the bull had moments earlier. He looked to Father for an explanation. "Where did that bull come from?"

Father pinched at the skin at his throat, pulling and releasing, pulling and releasing. Han wanted to reach up and make him stop. Father's blank stare filled Han with dread.

"Shìjiè mòrì le!" Father whispered. "It's the end of the world."

"No, it's not." He did not like Father this way—frightened and old looking. "We are alive. All these people are still alive."

Father's eyes snapped back into focus, and he turned to Han. "Yes, we are alive. The problem is the gōngniú is dead." He pointed at the bull.

"It's just a bull," Han said.

Father shook his head. "You know nothing of Chinese culture!" he scolded. "The earth rests on the back of four bulls. When the Earth Dragon trembled, the bulls escaped through the cracks in the earth. Now this one is dead." He spread out his hands, palms up. "How can the universe balance when the earth has lost its foundation?"

Han stared at Father in disbelief. An underground dragon? Four bulls that carried the world on their shoulders? Was any of this true?

"We must go to the temple and pray for the gods to put things right," Father said.

The temple of the goddess Tian Hou was only two blocks away. Han was stuck in the center of a crowd of worshippers headed in the same direction. Between their bodies, he caught glimpses of the earthquake's destruction.

Three horses were crushed under an avalanche of fallen bricks. Cable cars were tossed on their sides, tracks twisted as if squeezed by a giant hand. A room from the third floor of one building had fallen into the street. In the center of the wrecked room, a chair stood upright, a suit of clothing draped over its back as though this was any normal morning. From the exposed third floor, a man wrapped in a bedsheet called down, "Will someone please bring me my pants?"

No one volunteered.

As Han walked carefully around and over the giant gashes that cut through the street, his mind argued with itself.

There is no such thing as an Earth Dragon. Dragons are only in folktales.

How do you know? What if Father is right? What if this destruction is my fault?

He gnawed the inside of his cheek until blood filled his mouth.

Tian Hou Temple had survived the quake. Some of its ornate façade had broken, and the Chinese lanterns that dangled from the balcony now lay crushed in the street, but the building was intact. Han's shoulders relaxed a little. This had to be a good omen. He followed Father into the building.

The light was dim, and the air was thick with the scent of burning joss sticks. Dozens of Chinese lanterns dangled from the ceiling. Red cards attached to each lantern bore the name of the person who had donated to the temple on behalf of a dead relative. Somewhere up there was a lantern dedicated to Grandfather's memory.

The statue of Tian Hou presided in the middle of the altar, flanked by two lesser gods. Han stood back and watched Father perform the ritual.

First, Father kowtowed to the goddess three times, each bow respectfully low. Then he stepped to the side table and picked up the container of divinity sticks. Kneeling on the tile floor, he whispered a prayer too quietly for Han to hear.

Then Father shook the container until one stick fell out. He picked it up and read the numbers printed on the stick's side. Usually, a fortune-teller sat at the table to decipher the numbers. But today the table was empty, so Father looked up his fortune himself in the book of numbers.

Han rarely accompanied Father to the temple. All the bowing and kneeling and burning of paper prayers had seemed silly. He'd found it no different than Tom Sawyer trying to cure warts by throwing a dead cat at the devil in the graveyard at midnight. But maybe, in this upside-down world where an Earth Dragon trembled and bulls charged down city streets, Father knew what he was doing.

It took an eternity for Father to read his fate. When he finally closed the book and turned to Han, some of the lines in his forehead had softened.

"It is good news. The gods say . . ." Father closed his eyes and recited the words from memory. "'Why search in foreign lands for unknown gold? Like the man who holds the lamp and seeks for fire, pack your bags and set out for home.'"

Han must have looked confused, because Father smiled and patted him on the head. "This means the Earth Dragon has gone back to sleep. It is safe to go home."

Relief made Han's legs weak. Now they could return to the store and assess the damage. Life would get back to normal.

As Han stepped onto the sidewalk, something exploded in the distance. He flinched at the sound, but Father did not break stride. Han had to trot to keep up with him as he darted around fallen debris. Han's nose twitched. The air smelled smoky.

He glanced over his shoulder. They had just passed a woman cooking pancakes on a stove set up on the sidewalk. But the air smelled of burning chemicals, not food.

Another explosion boomed, closer this time. The nearer they got to the store, the more explosions Han heard. A black plume rose into the sky in the south, and a chill crept up the back of Han's neck. Could Father have misinterpreted his fortune? Those explosions sounded like a dragon's angry roar.

PROCLAMATION
FROM THE MAYOR OF SAN FRANCISCO

———— April 18, 1906 ————

It has come to my attention that thieves are taking advantage of San Francisco's current crisis to steal, plunder, loot, and commit other evil deeds. All police officers are hereby ordered to SHOOT TO KILL anyone caught looting or committing other serious crimes.

–*Mayor Eugene Schmitz*
Mayor of San Francisco

Chapter 6

April 18, 1906 — 10:00 a.m.

*H*an's cheeks grew hot at the sight of a pair of his underwear dangling from what remained of the ceiling in their bedroom. While he and Father had been in Portsmouth Square and the temple, aftershocks had further weakened the store. Its west side had collapsed, exposing their bedroom for the world to see.

Ignoring the danger, Father plunged into the wreckage. Han watched nervously as Father tossed aside planks and debris that covered his tipped-over desk. Then Father tugged at the top drawer where he kept important papers.

Han's belly growled loudly, a reminder that he had not eaten anything since those sugared almonds yesterday afternoon. He rummaged in the mess on the store's floor and found a carton of rice crackers, only partially crushed. Han gobbled down one packet and shoved six more in his pockets. But now he was thirsty. A crate of ginger ale contained three unbroken bottles. Han uncorked one and guzzled it down. Then he shoved the other two bottles under one arm and looked for other salvageable items.

Sitting atop a broken board, as if someone had put it there for safekeeping, was the basket that held Mother's things. It would make a handy carrying case. Han put the crackers and ginger ale inside. Then he found a coil of rope that he used to make a sling. He slipped his arms into two loops and swung the basket on his back.

"I can carry small things, Father," Han called.

Father was hunched over a drawer he had wrestled free from the desk.

A wagon carrying two soldiers came slowly up Dupont Street. Han supposed they were on rescue patrol, or maybe the wagon was to carry the dead. Despite the sun, a shiver ran through Han's body. He glanced outside at the handkerchief-covered face of Lung Tin. Someone had pulled the old man onto the sidewalk. Maybe the soldiers

could help transport his body somewhere safe until he could be buried.

"Excuse me," Han called as the wagon came closer. The soldier manning the reins had a clean-shaven face and looked quite young. He halted the horses next to Han. The second soldier had a bushy, rust-colored beard and looked a couple decades older. He stared at Han with eyes as hard as two blue pebbles.

"Get out of there!" the bearded man shouted.

Han jumped in alarm. "Out of where?" Then he realized the soldier was talking to Father.

"Hey, you!" the man yelled again. "Looting is illegal."

Father stared at the man and did not put down the papers he was holding. "I am not looting." Dislike dripped from his voice. "This is my property. These are my papers."

The bearded soldier hopped down from the wagon seat. He reached into the wagon and lifted out a rifle. Han's stomach dropped.

"The city is on fire, and everyone is being evacuated. You're ordered to head to the Presidio Army Base. Now move it."

Father straightened slowly. "I will leave as soon as I have what I need."

The soldier raised the gun to his shoulder. "If you think I'm going to stand here and let you steal, you're wrong."

The young soldier raised a calming hand. "Let's leave this, Clement. We've got to get these wounded folks to the Ferry Building so they can get on a boat to Oakland."

Han glanced in the wagon bed. Two women and a man lay there. A bone protruded from the man's leg, and both women had head wounds. Han turned away, feeling sick.

"I'm not stealing." Father's voice was hard. "This is my store, and I need my son's birth certificate and my identity papers."

The bearded soldier pulled back the bolt of the rifle. Han heard the click of a bullet fall into the chamber.

Time forgot all rules in the next few seconds. Han seemed to move in slow motion while everything around him sped up.

He stepped forward. "Leave the papers, Father!" The words oozed out like syrup.

The young soldier stood in the wagon seat and yelled, "Hold your fire, Clement!"

Father squatted down and returned to rummaging in the desk drawer.

CRACK!

The sound reverberated through Han's spine as though the bullet had struck him.

Father keeled over, one hand clasped to his side.

"I warned you!" the bearded soldier yelled. "Mayor's orders. Looters will be shot on sight!"

With a jolt, time returned to normal. Han darted toward Father, but the soldier stuck out his oak tree of an arm and blocked him. "Scram, kid, or I'll shoot you next."

"Father!" Han tried to duck under the arm.

The soldier shoved Han hard, and he fell to the ground. "I told you to beat it!"

Han ignored him. Scrambling to his feet, he darted around the soldier's legs and ran through the rubble to Father's side. Father's skin was the color of rice flour, and sweat beaded on his forehead. Father clutched his side with both hands, blood seeping between his fingers.

"Boy!" yelled the soldier. "You're asking for trouble."

Father's eyes were closed and his face twisted with pain. Han felt as helpless as he had yesterday when Elephant Ears had him by the queue, but this was worse. A million times worse.

"He's bleeding. Help him!" Han cried. "You have to help him!"

Father opened his eyes. "Kuài pǎo! Zhěngjiù nǐ zìjǐ," he whispered through clenched teeth.

Han shook his head violently. "No, Father, I will not run to save myself."

Father pleaded, his voice growing weak. "You must leave me, son. Get away from these men." He moaned.

Han patted the air frantically, afraid to touch Father for fear of hurting him. "What can I do to help? What can I do?"

Father raised one bloody hand and weakly pushed Han's arm. "Save yourself. You must obey me. Please, son. All that matters is for you to live. Save yourself."

Hot tears ran down Han's cheeks.

CRACK.

Another shot rang out, kicking up the dirt by Han's feet. He dove onto his belly. Cheek pressed into the ground, Han saw the bearded soldier ten feet away, rifle poised to shoot again.

"You got five seconds, kid," the man growled.

Han scrambled up. "But my father!"

"Four!"

Han looked from Father to the rifle and back to Father. "Three!"

The young soldier climbed down from the wagon's bench. "You're crazy, Clement. He's just a kid."

"Two!" The bearded soldier sighted his gun on Han.

"Duìbùqǐ!" The cry burst out of Han's mouth. "I'm sorry," he repeated in English.

Then Han ran.

Around the wagon. Over the crack in the road. Past the wreckage of the apothecary. In seconds, he was lost in the throng of refugees headed northwest toward the Presidio.

As he ran, the basket bumping against his back, Han pressed one fist against his chest. He felt like his ribs were about to cleave open and drop his heart on the ground. Was Father dying? Would Han ever see him again?

Nothing made sense.

The divinity stick had foretold that it was safe to go home. But home was more dangerous than the earthquake. And Father had said filial respect kept the universe in balance. But he had ordered Han to run away and save himself. A son did not show filial respect by abandoning his wounded father.

These thoughts ran in a loop through Han's mind as he raced down block after block.

Suddenly, Han skidded to a stop. People swarmed past him, bundles on their heads and children in their arms. Everyone was leaving Chinatown, but Han had to return. He could not just abandon Father. The thought of the bearded soldier with the rifle made him shiver with an icy sweat as he retraced his steps.

Han had reached the corner of Dupont and Jackson Streets, only two blocks from the store, when an explosion rocked the ground. Han dropped to his knees. That blast had been close. Too close. When the dust cleared, he ran down Dupont Street. But he did not get very far.

A cordon of soldiers stood where Washington Street intersected with Dupont. Han peered past the men. All he could see were flames and black smoke.

Han grabbed the arm of a passing Chinese man who was dragging a trunk by a rope. "What happened?" he asked, panic almost choking him.

"The Army is blowing everything up," the man said. "Get out of here!"

A silent sob started deep inside Han and became a howl. One of the soldiers turned and stared at him. The soldier had a beard and a rifle on his shoulder. Han clamped a hand over his mouth. Father was beyond his help now. Turning on his heel, Han ran.

April 18, 1906
8:00 a.m.

Message to: Acting Fire Chief John Dougherty
From: Presidio Army Base

Received your message that water mains are cracked and hydrants are empty. Understand that no water is available. The only solution, but it's dangerous, is to explode buildings to create firebreaks.

Have sent wagon with 48 barrels of black powder explosive to Fire Station 8. Have alerted all military posts and private gunpowder manufacturers in Bay Area to deliver available black powder and dynamite to nearest fire station.

Good luck.

Chapter 7

April 18, 1906 — 10:30 a.m.

*I*t was an obstacle course from a nightmare. Han splashed down alleyways flooded by broken water mains. He darted under dangling webs of electrical wires that spit angry fire at him. He climbed across wide fissures and over piles of debris. Buildings were twisted like corkscrews, and the sidewalks were like crumpled paper. And everywhere there were people.

Han tried not to look at the injured. When he saw a man trying to stanch a wound on his leg with a piece of ripped cloth, an image of Father's hands pressing against his side sprang unwanted into Han's mind. He raced past the wounded man.

The haze in the air grew thicker, and Han was forced to walk. The dirty air hurt his lungs. Ahead, flames licked the sides of a building. A fire wagon clattered past, its bell clanging a warning. The firefighters hooked their hose to the hydrant on the corner. But when they cranked the hydrant's valve open, water only dribbled out.

"Save it!" yelled a man who must have owned the building. "Find another hydrant."

The firefighter's expression looked defeated. "All the hydrants are dry. The earthquake broke the water pipes under the city."

"Do something!" the owner cried.

"We're doing our best," the firefighter said. "Fires are popping up all over the city. With no water, all we've got is dynamite."

"Dynamite!" The man was shouting now. "What good will that do?"

"To create firebreaks. The Army is trying to destroy buildings in the fire's path to starve the flames. Without fuel, they can't spread."

First an earthquake and now fire. Was this the Earth Dragon's wrath? Father would believe so. Han quickened his pace.

All that matters is that you live. Save yourself.

Han did not know if Father was alive or dead. All he could do now was honor Father's last request. To do that, he had to survive the Earth Dragon.

Everyone was fleeing downtown. Han passed an elderly man pushing a baby buggy that held an antique clock, two pots, and a lamp. A woman pulled a child's wagon with boxes teetering inside. Everywhere there were trunks. As people dragged them, the wooden or metal bottoms screeched against the cobblestone streets.

Han was walking next to an old Chinese woman and a girl of about nine, Meiying's age. The girl even resembled Han's sister. The same long black braid, the same button nose. Han slowed his pace to stay alongside her. The girl's likeness to Meiying comforted him, but also made his heart ache.

Was he going to have to write a letter to Mother and Meiying telling them that Father was dead? Shot in his own home? Burned when the Army blew up the block? Han swallowed a sob.

"Be careful, Grandmother," the girl said.

Han saw the old woman clutch at the girl's arm. The woman was tiny, but her weight was still too much for the thin girl to bear.

Without thinking, Han walked around the girl and offered his elbow to the woman. "May I help you?"

The grandmother's smile turned her face into a road map of wrinkles. She seized Han's arm and began to babble in rapid-fire Chinese. Her granddaughter, named Jun, had been at her house when the earthquake hit. They wanted to wait for Jun's parents to come and fetch them, but soldiers ordered them to leave Chinatown and go to the Presidio. The woman pointed down at her feet.

"The distance is far," she said.

Han looked down and realized the grandmother wore only stockings over twisted, tiny feet. His stomach churned. Mother was from a peasant family, and her feet were unbound. But she'd told Han about how the process worked for the daughters of wealthier families.

When a girl was only four or five years old, all toes but her big one were folded under her foot and wrapped with a cotton bandage. As the child grew, the bandages were tightened. Gradually, the heel moved forward toward the front of the foot. The bones in the arch were broken in the process. When the binding was complete, the girl would be given a small pair of shoes shaped like lotus blossoms.

Han had asked Mother why parents would hurt their daughters like this. Mother said Chinese women had been binding their feet for centuries. It was tradition and a status symbol among the rich. Mother said bound feet were not so very different from the tiny waists admired among upper-class American women. Women cinched their corsets so tight they could barely breathe.

Han now realized that a woman with bound feet walked very slowly. The grandmother was moving at a snail's pace, and Han wanted to speed up. Explosions were coming more frequently, not just from behind but to the west and east too. The air was hazy with smoke. It seemed like the Army's plan of fighting fire with fire was only feeding the Earth Dragon's rage.

Glancing behind him, Han saw ribbons of smoke stretching skyward. He counted sixteen in all. A piece of wood tripped the grandmother, and she would have toppled face-first in the street if Han had not caught her. His jaw clenched. If they did not quicken their pace, fire would soon surround them.

Jun bent over and began to cough. Her chest looked as frail as a bird's.

"We must rest," Han said. "Sit here."

Plastering on a reassuring smile, he led them to a beam on the sidewalk. Meanwhile, his brain worked frantically. He would distract them with crackers and ginger ale. Then he would abandon them.

Han could not meet the grandmother's eyes as he lowered her to the beam. With her tiny feet and Jun's scrawny legs, they would never outrun the Earth Dragon's fiery breath. But he dared not stay with them. He had to survive. He owed it to Father.

Jun stripped off her grandmother's torn stockings, and the old woman grimaced. Han avoided looking at her feet and removed the basket from his shoulders. He sat on the beam beside Jun and opened the basket and looked inside.

Han's breath caught in his throat. Inside the basket, resting against a bottle of ginger ale, was *Proverbs*. The hair on Han's arms rose. It was as if Father were there.

The grandmother let out a low moan. Jun held up one of her stockings. A piece of bloody skin clung to it.

Guilt stabbed Han again. He gave Jun and the grandmother his last two bottles of ginger ale and all the crackers. It was the least he could do. Before he left them to fend for themselves, maybe there was something in the basket for the grandmother's feet.

Rummaging around, Han found Mother's satin bridal slippers. Made of ruby-red cloth and embroidered with gold thread, the slippers were too fine and too big for the grandmother's twisted feet, but they were better than going barefoot. He gave the shoes to Jun. The girl's smile was so full of gratitude that Han had to look away.

As Han waited for the right moment to sneak away, he picked up *Proverbs*. A gust of wind fanned through the pages and the book fell open to a page labeled "Honesty."

Han's eyes fell on one line. As he read, he heard Father's voice in his mind.

True gold fears no fire.

But Han did fear fire. It was all around. His lungs breathed in its heat. His nose smelled its char. His ears heard its crackle.

Father had insisted these proverbs would guide Han in troubled times. Well, he was in trouble now, but this saying made no sense. Tears pricked the back of his eyes. He needed Father here, not some confusing book.

Angry, but desperate to feel Father's presence, Han read further.

One who tells true fortunes.

A good fellow will stick to his bargains.

Understanding slowly seeped in. Han's gaze returned to the first proverb. *True gold fears no fire.*

Han remembered Mr. Gao, the jeweler down the block, telling him that pure gold was too tough to melt in an ordinary fire. Only extreme heat altered pure gold's form. The proverb must mean that a pure person was like pure gold. When facing an ordeal, a pure person would stay true to what he knew was right. A pure person would not let his fear govern his actions.

Han snuck a glance at his companions. Jun tilted her head back and took a long swallow of ginger ale. The grandmother crossed her legs and smiled at her feet, now covered by the bright-red slippers. Was Han pure enough to help them instead of sneaking away to save himself?

A gust of wind sent smoke up Han's nose with the force of a punch. He slammed *Proverbs* shut and shoved it back into the basket. In his mind he yelled at Father. *I'm a human, not gold, and if I don't run soon, I'll burn to death alongside this old lady and girl!*

Springing to his feet, Han slung the basket over his shoulders.

"Time to go again?" Jun asked.

"Ah, um . . ." His mind froze. Scanning the surroundings, searching for an excuse for why he had to leave, his gaze fell on the handles of a wheelbarrow protruding from under a large beam in the ruins of a building across the street. An idea flashed in Han's mind, but there was one problem. He could not lift that beam by himself.

Three soldiers stood a short distance from the ruins. Memory of the rust-bearded soldier made Han hesitate. *True gold fears no fire.*

"Wait here," Han told Jun. "I'll be right back."

Han crossed the street and walked casually up to the soldiers, his hands in his pockets. "Excuse me."

The soldiers looked friendly enough.

"Is this Jacob Reinbach's house? You know," Han said, setting the bait, "the man with all those gold bars?"

The men exchanged looks. "Gold bars?" asked one. "What gold bars?"

Han knew Jacob Reinbach's house was blocks away, but he hoped these soldiers had never heard of the paranoid businessman Mr. Lock had talked about last night.

"You haven't heard about the gold bars he stores in his icebox?"

One soldier laughed. "No kidding?"

"No kidding," Han said. "I'm almost positive this was his house. His icebox must be under there somewhere." He pointed at the pile of debris.

The oldest-looking soldier scowled. "Looting is against the law. It can get you shot, kid."

The image of blood seeping between Father's fingers flashed through Han's mind. He shoved it aside. "Oh no, sir. I'd never steal. I just thought since you're soldiers, you maybe should remove the gold for safekeeping. Before somebody else steals it."

The men shared a meaningful look. "Kid's got a point," said one.

"Yes, he does," said another man, grinning broadly.

They had taken the bait. Now Han just needed to reel them in.

"If you help me uncover this wheelbarrow, you can fill it with rubble and I'll haul it away. It'll make digging out the icebox quicker." A look of suspicion crossed the oldest soldier's face, and Han quickly added, "It'll only cost you a nickel per load."

The oldest soldier grinned. "Leave it to a Chinese kid to do business in a disaster."

Han forced his mouth into a grin.

"It's a deal," said the soldier.

The three men easily freed the wheelbarrow and quickly loaded it full of debris. The oldest soldier tossed a nickel to Han and told him to dump the load across the street beside a large pile of rubble.

"I'll be right back," Han said.

As he pushed the heavy load across the street, Han glanced over his shoulder. The soldiers were digging through the remains, looking for an icebox. Han had to hurry in case they found one and discovered it only held spoiled milk and broken eggs.

He dumped the rubble and raced the wheelbarrow over to the grandmother and Jun. "We have transportation," he said. Without asking permission, Han scooped up the grandmother and set her in the wheelbarrow. "Now you," he ordered Jun. She climbed in and nestled between her grandmother's legs.

Heading down a side street at a trot, Han braced himself for a shout from the soldiers. It never came. They were too busy looking for fool's gold.

Han was hot, thirsty, and frightened. But as he wheeled his cargo away, he chuckled. That was a trick right out of

The Adventures of Tom Sawyer. When Tom's aunt ordered him to paint a fence, he pretended the job was so much fun that all his friends begged to do it. So, Tom charged them. He got rich and the fence got painted. Han got a wheelbarrow and a nickel.

Maybe deceiving those soldiers was not the act of someone who was "true gold," but he had not abandoned the grandmother and Jun. Also, he was still trying to save himself so he could keep his promise to Father. Was that enough filial piety to make the Earth Dragon happy? Would it go away and set the world right again? As if in answer, another explosion shook the ground.

Chapter 8

April 18, 1906 — 6:00 p.m.

$\mathcal{T}$wenty-three blocks later, Han wheeled the grandmother and Jun through the gates of the Presidio Army Base. His legs throbbed, and blisters burned on both heels. Hundreds of tents dotted the grassy plain around the military barracks.

A guard at the gate stopped Han. "Family units are being housed over there." He pointed past the last row of barracks. "The army tents are small, but you three will fit. Your tent number is 678."

Han pushed the wheelbarrow past a long line of people waiting outside a kitchen tent. The smell of roasted meat and vegetables made his mouth water. The people waiting for food were all white. The Chinese stood in groups off to the side, as if afraid to get in the line. Suddenly, the grandmother cried out and tried to stand in the wheelbarrow.

"Whoa!" Han stopped. "You're going to tip it."

The old woman scrambled out and hobbled toward a group of Chinese people, her red slippers flapping out like duck feet.

Then Jun cried, "Papa!" She hopped out of the wheelbarrow too. A tall man dressed in a western shirt and pants dropped to his knees and swept Jun into his arms.

A shameful jealousy crept over Han as he watched them embrace. It was good that Jun and the grandmother had been reunited with their family. Still, he would give anything to see Father emerge from the crowd. But that was not going to happen. Han turned to head in the direction where his tent should be.

"Děng děng!" The old woman called to Han to wait.

The man walked over to him, the grandmother on his arm. She introduced the man as her son, and she told her son how Han had carried her and Jun all the way from Chinatown.

The man bowed low. "You have aided my mother and daughter. I don't know how to repay you."

Shame burned Han's cheeks. What would this man say if he knew Han had wanted to abandon them?

"My mother invites you to come and stay in our tent," the man continued. He forced a laugh. "With me, my wife, three sons, and now my daughter and mother."

Han understood. The man was thankful, but there was no room for him in their tiny tent.

"Thank you for your kindness, but I have been assigned a tent."

The man smiled gratefully, but the grandmother scowled. In Chinese she said, "This boy is alone. He must come with us."

Her son muttered, "He'll be fine. He's practically a man."

Han straightened his back. He did not feel like a man, but he would act like one. He pushed the wheelbarrow forward. "Take this. You need it more than I do."

The grandmother took Han's hands in hers. Pulling him down to her height, she embraced him. "To save one man's life is better than to build a seven-story pagoda," she whispered.

Han hugged her back and thought that Father would like this old woman. Waving goodbye to Jun, Han headed to his tent.

When he crawled inside tent 678, he was relieved he had not taken the grandmother up on her offer. These military tents were built for only two men. Outside, the wind blew in strong gusts. Distant explosions boomed, making Han jump. Each breath tasted of ash.

Removing the basket, Han sat on the floor of the tent and tried to figure out what he was supposed to do now. His mind was blank, so he opened the basket to see if it held any other treasures.

Han pulled out Mother's wooden moon-cake mold. He closed his eyes and pretended the family was together in their old apartment celebrating the Moon Festival. The kitchen smelled of the sweet pastry and lotus-seed filling. After dinner, they each got a slice of cake, and then they joined their neighbors on the streets to gaze up at the full moon. When Grandfather was alive, he'd told stories of their Chinese ancestors. Would the family ever gather again for such an occasion? A pang of sorrow shot through Han.

He returned the pastry mold to the basket and looked to see what else the container held. He took out *Proverbs* and set it on the floor beside him, then pulled out two of Mother's aprons and an old shirt of Father's that needed mending. He held these to his nose and inhaled. It was probably just his imagination, but under the smoky air, Han thought he detected a hint of the jasmine tea Father loved and Mother's favorite sandalwood scent.

At the bottom of the basket, Han found a twisted butterfly shaped from red cord. He smiled, remembering how Father tried to teach Meiying to tie the decorative knots that were a Chinese art form. His sister had been so proud of this deformed little butterfly. Finding these personal items made Han feel somehow more hopeful, like maybe there was a chance that Father had survived and the family would be reunited someday.

Han returned everything to the basket except *Proverbs*. He flipped through the book, sentences flying by in a blur.

Suddenly, a scream pierced the night, sending a bolt of terror through him. He leaped to his feet, shoved the book in his pocket, and ran outside.

Another shriek exploded from the tent next to Han's. Without hesitating, he entered the untied flap door. On a cot in the middle of the tent, a white woman lay with her knees drawn up. A blanket covered the unmistakable bulge of her balloon-sized belly.

The woman stretched out one arm toward Han. "Help me!"

He watched in horror as she twisted in pain. "Oh no, sorry, lady." Han backed toward the tent door. "I don't know anything about babies."

Tipping her head back and gritting her teeth, she bellowed like a cow, the cords on her neck popping out. Han froze in place. The woman's roar seemed endless.

Finally, she fell back on the cot. Then, to Han's astonishment, the woman laughed. "I don't need you to deliver this baby," she said, wiping sweat from her forehead. "I need you to put that out." The woman nodded at the tent ceiling.

Han looked up. A tongue of flame was licking the seam that ran down the roof's center.

"Oh no!" He reeled back in alarm. "I'll get some water."

Han raced between the rows of tents, asking everyone where he could find water. Finally, a man pointed to a large barrel that stood next to the army barracks, several buckets on the ground beside it. Han filled two buckets with water and hurried back to the tent.

The woman's bellows had turned into doglike panting sounds. Han did not dare peek inside to see what had changed. Instead, he doused the roof with water and raced off to fill the buckets again.

Four more times, Han filled and emptied the buckets. The fire had been extinguished by the second bucket, but Han needed to feel like he was helping in some way. When he returned for the fourth time, a man emerged from the tent. Beyond him, Han saw a doctor from Presidio's hospital speaking to the woman on the cot.

"My wife told me what you did. What a great kid you are." The man pumped Han's hand up and down. "How can I thank you?"

"That's alright," Han said. "I'm glad I found water."

The man fished in his pocket and pulled out a fifty-cent piece. "Please take this. You saved my wife." Just then, they heard a baby wail from inside the tent.

The man locked eyes with Han and grinned widely. "And you saved my baby too." He swept Han up in a bear hug, lifting him off the ground. Then, setting Han down and pressing the coin into Han's hand, the man said, "I gotta go see what it is." He entered the tent.

A warm glow filled Han. The man's joy was contagious. Plus, Han felt proud. If he had not put out that fire, who knows what would have happened to the woman and her baby?

"Whooee!" the man yelled. "It's a boy!"

Tossing the fifty-cent piece into the air, Han called out, "Heads." His luck was going to change. He could feel it. The Earth Dragon was going to retreat back underground where it belonged.

Snatching the coin out of the air, Han opened his fist.

It had landed on tails.

Han shrugged it off. Just a silly coin toss. It did not mean anything. He returned the buckets to the water barrel and walked slowly to his tent. Fatigue fell over him like a heavy blanket. All he wanted was to curl up on the floor of the tent and fall asleep.

Tomorrow the fires would be out. Tomorrow he could hunt for Father. Tomorrow he could figure out what the future held. Tonight he must rest.

Upon entering the tent, Han immediately knew something was wrong. It was the same empty space with nothing but canvas walls and a canvas floor. That was it! The tent should not have been empty. While he had been helping put out the fire on his neighbor's tent, someone had stolen the basket.

The theft hit Han like an ax-head striking granite. It shattered his bones and made sparks fly from behind his eyelids. It knocked loose a wedge of something inside him. He collapsed to the floor and sobbed.

The basket was the absence of Mother and Meiying. It was the store, first broken and now burned. It was the queue Han had tossed at Father last night and the words he had hurled that he could not take back. It was the regret Han felt that he had not apologized to Father. It was Han's fear that now it was too late.

Han did not know how long he wept, but finally his tears ran dry. He rolled onto his back and stared at the tent roof. But he could not get comfortable, because something was digging into his back. Han reached under him and pulled out the book of proverbs from his back pocket.

He still had this one piece of his family. Desperate for comfort, Han turned the pages slowly and read.

An anxious individual is one who is afraid his bones will decay before he is dead.

The word "decay" sent a shiver up Han's spine, and he flipped the page.

The melon seller declares his melons sweet.

Han shook his head. That was no help. He turned the page again.

To rush on the foe at the point of the spear is the mark of a truly brave man.

Han squeezed his eyes shut in frustration. He could not use a spear to defeat the vengeance of the Earth Dragon. Earlier, when he was with Jun and her grandmother, Father had whispered the proverb about true gold in his mind. These silly sayings were just words on paper. Han needed to hear Father's voice again.

He turned the pages quickly, frantically. Then his eyes fell on a familiar proverb, one Father recited when Han complained about difficult homework. In his mind, Father's voice spoke.

Without climbing the mountains no one can know the height of heaven, and without diving streams no one can know the thickness of the earth.

Han knew what this proverb meant. If he wanted something, he had to work for it.

Han sat up. He did want something. He wanted to find his father. Ignoring his tired legs and burning blisters, Han stood, wiped his eyes, shoved *Proverbs* into his back pocket, and headed out into the night.

April 19, 1906
San Francisco Examiner

CHINATOWN NO MORE

The Army's effort to create a firebreak along Kearny Street has destroyed Chinatown. After running out of stick dynamite, officials used black powder, a flammable powder hard to control.

On Wednesday, April 18, soldiers blew up a building on the corner of Kearny and Clay streets. However, the wind picked up bedding from that building and sent it sailing across the street. The flaming sheets ignited structures on the edge of Chinatown. By 2:00 a.m. on Thursday, all of Chinatown was ablaze.

As this paper goes to press, much of San Francisco is in flames.

Chapter 9

April 18, 1906 — 10:00 p.m.

*W*ater. Han needed it, desperately. Not only was his throat a desert, but San Francisco was an inferno and growing hotter by the minute. When Han had left the Presidio hours earlier, he'd been determined not to stop walking until he found Father. But as night descended and the sky turned red, he realized the search was impossible until the city stopped burning.

Han wandered up one block and down the next, looking for the waterfront. The ocean was the only place where he would feel safe from the fiery breath of the Earth Dragon. Ash fell from the sky. The streets were much less crowded than earlier, but the people who were out looked as exhausted as Han felt.

Just when Han was about to collapse from thirst, he heard piano music and a man singing. Turning the corner, he discovered a makeshift camp on the sidewalk. A white woman, arms the size of salted hams, stirred something in a washbasin atop a wood stove. The smell of the basin's contents made Han's mouth water. A man in a bowler hat plunked out a song on a nearby piano, a young girl beside him. Several people were squeezed onto a couch, and a few more lay on a nearby bed. Han felt like he should avert his gaze. The inside lives of San Franciscans were on display.

Han was not the only person drawn by the sounds and smells of the makeshift camp. A girl walked up to the woman at the stove and held out a tin can.

"Momma asks if you'll take ground coffee for some soup."

"Sounds like a fair trade," the woman said. She dumped the coffee from the girl's can into a kettle boiling on the stove and then ladled soup into the can and handed it back to the girl. The girl disappeared down the street.

A man passing by pulled three potatoes and an onion from a sack over his shoulder. "I'll add these to the pot if I can stay long enough to have a bite," he said.

"Thank you kindly," the woman replied. She began to clean the potatoes.

Han was so thirsty his tongue was pasted to the roof of his mouth. But everyone in the camp was white, and they seemed to be operating by trade. Would they welcome a Chinese boy with nothing to offer? His brain told him not to take the chance, but his thirst ordered his feet to cross the street.

Han slunk silently up to the stove. The woman gave him a knowing look.

"Hungry, boy?" she asked.

"Thirsty," he croaked.

"Water is as scarce as hen's teeth. What have you got to trade?"

"Nothing."

The woman sighed and rested her hands on her hips. "If we just go giving out something for nothing, soon we'll all have nothing. You must have something to share?"

Was she blind? He was just a boy dressed in filthy clothes. Other than the fifty-cent piece and the nickel, the only possession he had in the entire world was the book of proverbs in his pocket. Han knew he would need the money, and the woman could not toss the book of proverbs into her soup pot. Even if she wanted it, Han would not part with the book. It was his last piece of Father. Then Han had an idea. The woman did not seem unkind. Perhaps . . .

"I can share wisdom," Han said.

The woman drew back. "Wisdom? I can't eat wisdom, boy."

"The mind needs wisdom to survive as much as the body needs food," he said.

A slow smile spread across the woman's broad face. "Alright, what wisdom have you got that's worth some soup and a cup of water?"

Han's mind raced. He had not read much of *Proverbs*, but Father was constantly reciting these sayings. He considered and rejected several phrases before selecting one he hoped would appeal to the woman.

Han cleared his throat, looked directly into the woman's eyes, and recited, "'Who constantly gives, does always possess. His riches and honors never grow less.'"

The woman cocked her head and considered him. "Hm. Sounds like something my preacher might say. Do good and good will come back to you."

"Yes," Han said. "My father always says this."

"Where's your pa now?"

Han's mouth quivered, and he did not trust himself to speak. He just shrugged one shoulder in the direction of Chinatown.

Pity flashed across the woman's face. "I can always use more wisdom. You got yourself a trade, boy."

So Han found himself sitting on the grass, a tin can of water in one hand and a jar of soup in the other. While he ate and drank, the piano man sang, "It's going to be a hot time in the old town tonight."

When Han finished his meal, the woman pointed in the direction of the waterfront, and he began to walk again. After a few blocks, he found himself in front of the wrought iron gates of the Laurel Hill Cemetery. In the red light cast by the glow of the distant fire, Han saw a field of grass dotted with tombstones. Suddenly, exhaustion swept over him. The fire seemed far away. The cemetery was quiet, and the grass would make a soft bed. He walked through the gates.

Many tombstones had toppled over or cracked in half. The earthquake had even spit some coffins right out of the ground. Han found an intact tombstone. It was too dark to read the engraving, but moss on the stone reassured him the grave was old. He did not want to sleep over the body of someone who had died recently.

Leaning back against the tombstone, Han's limbs tingled with relief. He was so tired. Images of the terrible day flitted through his mind. The twisted earth. Lung Tin's cracked skull. Blood seeping between Father's fingers. But his exhausted body forced Han into sleep.

THUNK! CRACK! THUD!

Han bolted upright. For a moment, he was back in bed, and the Earth Dragon was trembling again. Then he felt the grass under his hands and remembered. Whispered voices drifted from several yards away. Han shivered in an icy sweat and shrank back against the tombstone. Was this graveyard haunted?

Then two men appeared, shadowy figures bending over a coffin a few graves away. One man jammed a crowbar under the coffin lid and leaned on it. With a sharp crack, the lid unsealed. The second man lifted the lid.

Han dropped flat on his back. Were these men corpse-stealers like the doctor who was murdered in *The Adventures of Tom Sawyer*? His legs twitched. He wanted to run, but who knew what these men would do to a witness? So he stayed perfectly still.

"Get his watch," one man whispered. "That'll fetch a couple bucks."

"It ain't gold," said the other man. "Silver maybe."

Not body-stealers, then. Just ordinary thieves.

"Still," said the first man, "we're getting a decent haul tonight."

The second man chuckled. "Too bad we can't have earthquakes more often. Didn't even need a shovel tonight."

"Hey, look there," said the first man. "That body got tossed clear out of its coffin, and it looks to be a fresh one."

Han's heart froze. He had been spotted. Willing himself not to breathe, not to blink, not to twitch, Han played dead.

Footsteps padded closer. A hot blast of onion breath made Han's nostrils quiver.

"This one is just a kid," said the second man.

A hand rifled through Han's pockets and pulled out *Proverbs*.

"Nothing in his pocket but this stupid book."

The onion breath came closer. "Aw, this is a waste of time. He ain't nothing but a Chinese boy," said the first man.

A grunt from the other man signaled he had stood up. "Those gal-dang rat-eaters are everywhere these days."

"Don't surprise me to find rat-eaters in a graveyard though," said the first man. "Probably good hunting ground."

Anger flashed through Han like a lightning bolt. In his mind, Father recited the proverb Han had dismissed back in the tent at the Presidio. But Father was not whispering now. He was shouting.

To rush on the foe at the point of the spear is the mark of a truly brave man.

Han opened his eyes. "I am the Earth Dragon!" he bellowed.

The first thief shrieked and fell back on his rear.

"What the heck!" barked the second man. He darted behind a nearby tomb.

Han sprang to his feet, grabbed the book, and ran. He leaped over tombstones, darted around mausoleums, raced out the gates of the cemetery, and kept running.

Finally, when he could run no more, Han stopped in the shadow of a building that had survived the earthquake. He pressed himself against the wall and peeked behind him. The street was empty.

As Han struggled to catch his breath, he recalled the image of the thief's face when he had yelled. The man's eyes had bulged in fright. He'd looked like he had seen a ghost. Han began to laugh. The thief had fallen backward on his bottom, legs up in the air like a capsized beetle. Han laughed harder. It felt good to laugh. Even Tom Sawyer had not been brave enough to confront the villains in the graveyard. Han could not wait to tell Father about this.

With that thought, his laughter fell silent. He turned to face downtown San Francisco. Over the city center, flames spiraled into the sky, and smoke billowed in angry puffs. One tongue of fire darted this way and that, seeming to taste the air. The Earth Dragon was still on the hunt, and Han could not shake the feeling that it would not rest until it devoured him. After all, it was Han's fault that the dragon had awoken.

If Han was going to survive, he had to get out of San Francisco until the fire was extinguished. For that, he needed a boat. Turning away from the flames, Han resumed his search for the sea.

Chapter 10

April 19, 1906 — 12:00 a.m.

Just when Han was about to give up and collapse in the nearest doorway, he saw a golden glow bobbing in the distance. He stumbled toward it. As the light grew bigger, Han heard the slap of waves against rocks. A few more steps and he was there—the waterfront.

The light came from a lantern on a tugboat docked at the pier. Shadowed by darkness, Han watched three men unload crates from the boat and put them into a wagon.

The lantern beckoned to Han. It was a warm, golden light, unlike the Earth Dragon's angry red eye that loomed over the center of the city. The crew finished moving the crates and the men leaned against the wagon, their backs to the dock. One man lit a cigarette. Another pointed at the

San Francisco Bay. Han mentally traced his escape route. With the Earth Dragon's fiery breath drawing closer, Han had to get out of San Francisco.

On feet as silent as cats' paws, Han darted up the dock and vaulted over the boat's railing. The gleam of the lantern directed him into the boat's small forecastle. Padded benches were attached to the walls. A small stove stood in one corner, a table in the other. Han crawled underneath the table, curled into a ball, and fell instantly asleep.

Time passed. Minutes. Hours. Han did not know. All he knew was that suddenly he was awake and afraid. He took in his surroundings. The planks of the wooden floor felt rough underneath his cheek. Overhead, a spider dangled from a web in one corner of the wooden table. The cabin smelled like strong coffee. A rolling sensation told Han the vessel was at sea. Three pairs of boots stood around the table—with legs inside them.

Han's pulse quickened. Last night he had only cared about escaping the burning city. His sleep-deprived brain had not considered what would happen if he was discovered aboard. He raced through his options.

Run up on deck and jump overboard.

But he could drown.

Curl up and play dead.

But if the crew discovered him, they would toss him overboard. And he could drown.

Before Han could think of a third option, a big hand reached under the table, grabbed him by the tunic, and hauled him to his feet.

The hand was attached to a white man. He was short, with a chest as round and sturdy as a barrel of rice. Han glanced from side to side. Another white man stood on his left, and a third was on his right. He was surrounded.

"Who are you?" asked the barrel-chested man. "And what are you doing on this boat?"

"I had to escape the Earth Dragon." Han knew immediately by the expressions on the sailors' faces that these words were a mistake. The men burst into laughter.

"Personally, I'm more afraid of witches than dragons," said the tall man on Han's left. "What about you, James?"

"Well, Leon, actually it's Frankenstein's monster that gets me every time," said the third man. He wiggled his body in a fake shiver.

The barrel-chested man grabbed the back of Han's neck. Not hard, but with enough pressure to show he meant business. Steering him out the door, the man said, "Let's find the captain."

Out on deck, Han realized that morning had arrived. A sickly light fell across everything. The sun was a tiny bloodred circle, trying in vain to push through the smoke. When Han caught sight of the harbor, he gasped.

The tugboat was only a few hundred yards from shore in front of the Ferry Building, San Francisco's main hub for water transportation. A 300-foot-long grain barge was moored alongside the dock. People, as thick as ants, crowded the dock, trying to claim a spot on the barge. Behind them, the city burned.

A tugboat, no bigger than the one Han rode, was pushing another grain barge loaded with passengers through the choppy waves toward Oakland, which lay across the bay. Small vessels of every kind, from sailboats

to rowboats to launch boats to skiffs, were ferrying people to several luxury ocean liners anchored in the harbor.

A woman stood at the bow of the tugboat, her back facing Han. He glanced up at the bridge, the small cabin where the captain steered the vessel. But it was empty.

"We got a stowaway, Captain," announced the barrel-chested man.

The woman turned around. Wavy brown hair framed a face with a nose so sharp it cut the face in two. Han looked around. There was no one else there.

"You can look at me, boy," the woman said. "I'm Captain Eliza Thorrold."

Han widened his eyes.

The captain made a face. "Don't wet your pants. I may be one of the only licensed female boat pilots on this coast, but I'm more than competent."

Han swallowed and nodded.

"Now what the devil are you doing on the *Ethel and Marion*? We are in the middle of ferrying supplies and people out of that inferno." She jerked her head in the direction of the shore.

"He said he had to get away from the Earth Dragon," said Leon with a snort.

The captain nodded slowly, but she did not laugh like the sailors. "Dey loong jun. I've heard the Chinese yelling about the Earth Dragon trembling."

Leon looked at the captain, his eyebrows drawn clear up to his forehead. "You mean to tell me there's actually a real dragon?"

She gave him a look of disgust. "Of course not. Earthquakes are caused by geology." The captain moved her hands around in the air. "Something about one piece of bedrock banging against another piece of bedrock when Earth's core heats up. A friend of my dear departed husband was a scientist, and he liked to talk about how dangerous it was to live in San Francisco. During the gold rush, folks were so hungry for land they filled in part of the bay with all kinds of junk—rotten wood, dirt, and whatnot." She gestured to the burning city. "A city built on a landfill doesn't hold up well when the bedrock starts to shift."

Bedrock. Geology. Earth's core.

Han stared past the captain to the smoldering city. All of a sudden, the fire transformed. It still looked powerful and dangerous, but it felt different. Geology was not personal. Earth's core was not hunting him. The earthquake was a natural disaster. The fire was its consequence. Han had not caused either event. He did not know if he felt like laughing or crying.

"Now, I don't have time to give you a science lesson, kid. And I don't have time to deal with a stowaway. Should I just toss you overboard? Explain yourself."

The disappearance of the Earth Dragon took Han's fear with it. His mind was clear and sharp as it searched for a way out of the fix he was in. A strong wind buffeted him, and Han grabbed the railing. The breeze carried Father's voice.

Borrow the wind to cross the river.

As a businessman, Father was always on the lookout for opportunity. Just last week, an order for ten barrels of dried oysters had arrived as fresh oysters. Father marked them on sale and sent Han out on the sidewalk to convince all passersby that they needed fresh oysters. "Borrow the wind to cross the river" meant that when a problem came up, one should use it to his advantage. The oysters had all sold.

Han had an opportunity right here. All he had to do was seize it.

"My name is Han Liu," he said, throwing his shoulders back and standing up tall. "I have a business proposition for you."

The rumor of a grin appeared on the captain's mouth. She raised one eyebrow and waited.

Han continued. "I climbed aboard your boat to escape the Earth Drag—I mean, the fire. It's still too dangerous to return, and I don't want you to toss me overboard."

The captain folded her arms and waited some more.

"Instead of drowning me, put me to work."

She frowned. "I already have Leon,"—she pointed at the tall man—"Martin,"—she pointed at the barrel-chested sailor—"and James." She indicated the third man. "I don't have the budget or space for anyone else. Besides, how old are you? Like ten?"

Han scowled. "I'm twelve. Anyway, I'll work for free. I'll do any chores you want. I can sleep on the deck, and I only want to stay aboard until the fire is out."

"No pay at all?" The captain looked like she did not believe him.

Han shrugged. "Well, I would like one favor."

"Here it comes," said Leon.

Han shot him a dirty look. "All I ask is that after the fire is out, you put me ashore in the best place possible to get information about what happened to my father."

The captain shared a look with her crew. "When did you last see your father?" she asked.

The dark memory descended upon Han. The bearded soldier. The gunshot. Father falling. Blood seeping from between his fingers. *All that matters is that you live.*

Around the boulder of sorrow that sat in Han's throat, the tale poured out. Even his cracked lips and dry throat could not stop the flow of words. The captain and crew listened in silence.

When he had finished, Han leaned against the railing. His legs were calling it quits. "So I don't know if Father is dead or alive. But I cannot rest until I find him." He gazed over the railing into the murky blue-green waters of the bay. "Or until I find his body."

He turned to meet the captain's gaze. "It's my duty, you see, as his son. I must care for my father. Even after death." His voice cracked on the last word.

"Here, kid." Leon handed Han a mug of water. "After a night like that, I'll bet you're thirsty."

Thus, Han Liu became a temporary deckhand aboard the *Ethel and Marion*. The captain told him she would not make false promises. She did not know how, or if, San Francisco could account for all the missing and dead after a disaster like this one. But she promised to drop him off someplace where he might find answers.

For the next three days, as the fire department and Army gradually put out the flames, Han worked. He made sandwiches and coffee, dumped the chamber pot, coiled rope, cleaned hoses, mopped the deck, and hauled boxes, and every time the tugboat pushed a barge loaded with refugees from the Ferry Building to Oakland, he scrutinized each face. None belonged to Father.

SAN FRANCISCO CHRONICLE

April 25, 1906

PLAN FOR A NEW CHINATOWN

The fire has erased Chinatown from central San Francisco and city fathers are determined to keep it that way. The mayor's office has announced that a new Chinatown will be constructed at Hunters Point, on the extreme southern edge of the county.

When officials were asked if the Chinese approved of this relocation, considering they will be leaving prime real estate in downtown to be banished to the outskirts of the city, a representative of the mayor said, "No comment."

Chapter 11

April 30, 1906

For nine never-ending days, Han paced the Presidio refugee camp. He did not blame Captain Thorrold for the fact that he was trapped in the remote corner of the peninsula. When the official announcement came on Saturday, April 21, that San Francisco had stopped burning, the captain had deposited Han at the Presidio's pier. If anyone could track down the injured, wounded, or dead, surely it was the United States Army.

Having grown fond of Han over his three-day stint as deckhand, the crew passed around a hat and collected $17.32 for him. Captain Thorrold wrote her address on a card and said that once Han got his affairs settled, if he wanted a life on the sea, he should get in touch. There would always be a job on the *Ethel and Marion* for him. She said Han represented the American spirit—tough, resilient, and brave.

When Han watched the tugboat steam away from the Presidio's pier, loneliness swelled up inside him. He liked the crew and the captain, but he did not want a life on the sea. He wanted his family back.

Determined to discover what happened to Father, Han went to the base's main office to ask questions. He found no answers. Instead, he was assigned another tiny tent and housed beside the other Chinese refugees in the windiest corner of the base. A forty-year-old man shared Han's tent. He had been trapped under his house during the earthquake. The man had escaped major injury, but woke every night screaming from nightmares.

At first, Han was thankful to have a roof over his head. But gratitude became frustration when he tried to leave camp to look for Father on his second day there. Guards at the front gates stopped him. No civilians were permitted into the city yet, they said. It was still too dangerous.

So Han bided his time, reading *Proverbs* and walking the rocky shoreline from one end of the Presidio to the other.

Then, on his seventh day at camp, while standing in line to use the latrine, Han heard a rumor. While the Chinese were still denied entrance to the city, white people were looting Chinatown. The curious, the souvenir seekers, even National Guardsmen were digging through the wreckage of Chinese homes and businesses searching for silver, bronze, jade, or porcelain that had survived the disaster.

After using the bathroom, Han ran to the front gate. He told the guards that the Liu Grocery & Dry Goods store had no precious items. Looters could take anything they wanted. He just needed to go home to find his father.

Not yet, said the guards.

Han wanted to pummel them, kick them, and run past their rifles. Instead, he bit his tongue, returned to the tent, and reread the proverb he had discovered that was helping him endure.

Forbearance under a slight provocation may save one hundred days of trouble.

Being trapped in the Presidio was not a "slight provocation," but Han knew fighting the guards would not get him any closer to finding Father.

Finally, on April 30, ten days after the last fire in the city had finally been extinguished, camp officials announced that the Chinese could go investigate their property. Han was the first one out of the gates.

The deeper into the city he walked, the more he was struck by the terrible beauty of the ruins. The fire must have

been so hot that it consumed its own charcoal. Left in the fire's wake were crumbled iron, brick, and marble in pastel shades of mauve, fawn, and pink. San Francisco looked like a city out of the history books from one thousand years ago. But the otherworldly loveliness made Han feel worse, not better. The destruction was so complete.

Tents and shanties lined the streets. These structures were cobbled together from salvaged items like warped corrugated iron, doors pulled from wrecked buildings, and window shutters, coats, and bedspreads.

When Han reached Chinatown, he found the neighborhood surrounded by heavy wire and manned by an armed guard. The government had finally decided to prevent more looting. Han showed the permit that allowed him to pass through.

Liu Grocery & Dry Goods was nothing but rubble and ash. For days, Han had prepared himself for this sight, but the reality of it was a blow that almost sent him to his knees. He scanned the destruction, hoping for some sign of Father. There was nothing but charred boards and soot.

So Han dug.

He found a bone button, broken shards of china, and a hammer. He did not find Father.

Sitting back on his haunches, Han wiped the sweat off his brow. It was hopeless. He must accept that Father was dead—by the soldier's bullet or by the fire. What did the cause of death matter anymore? Father was dead. But without a body, how could Han give him a proper burial? He had failed in his final duty of filial respect.

As it did every night in his dreams, the scene of that terrible morning replayed in Han's mind. The bearded soldier. The gunshot. Father falling.

"Forgive me," Han whispered.

Then he heard it. Father's voice. Not faint and trembling as it had been that horrible morning, but clear and strong. *All that matters is that you survive.*

These had been Father's last words. His last request of his son.

Han plunged his hands into the still-warm ash. He had fulfilled Father's request. He had used the knowledge of the proverbs and his own wits, and he had survived. The Earth Dragon trembled, the Earth Dragon breathed fire, the Earth Dragon pushed him into the sea, but Han had discovered there was no Earth Dragon. He had survived and the dragon had vanished. In surviving, Han had given Father all the filial respect he was able to give.

Now there was nothing to do but trek back to the Presidio and perform the task he had been dreading: writing a letter to Mother and Meiying to tell them Father was dead. Then he had to figure out how he was to live. In his pocket, he carried the money the crew had given him, the card with Captain Thorrold's address, and *Proverbs*. This was all he owned in the world.

The time had come to leave. Han took one last look, trying to resurrect the memory of what had once been his home. In his mind, Father stood behind the counter, sipping a cup of jasmine tea. Meiying and Han sat side by side at the table, Meiying teasing him as she liked to do. Mother restocked shelves as she entertained them with a funny story about a chicken on the loose at the market.

But today, the sun was too bright for the memory to stick. It illuminated the ugly gray truth in front of Han. As he turned away, sunlight glinted off something under a charred beam. Han walked into the wreckage of what had been the center of the store.

Under the beam was the copper wok that Father had cooked supper in the night before the quake. It was upside down. The fire had turned the copper green except for one small circle that shone like a spotlight in the sunbeam.

Han pulled out the wok from under the wood. He flipped it over. There sat Father's mahjong dice and the frizzled remains of Han's queue. He picked up the dice and shook them in his palm. Father loved to play mahjong. Actually, he loved to win mahjong. The dice felt warm, almost like Father's hand was in his.

Han picked up the queue. This frizzled and charred braid had represented Han as a Chinese boy. It had meant so much to Father and been so hated by Han. He had insisted that he was an American boy, and he was. But now Han understood. He was Chinese too.

American. Chinese. American Chinese. Chinese American. Han was both things, at once. Two parts of one whole.

An ache swelled inside of him. How could any boy, whether Chinese or American or anything else, survive without his family, Father dead and Mother and Meiying thousands of miles away? Han needed to begin life over, but doubted he had the strength to do it alone.

"Han Liu! Han Liu!"

The sound of his name startled Han. He looked up to see Mr. Sing running toward him.

"You are alive, Han Liu!" The herbalist hauled Han to his feet and hugged him tightly. "Your father will be overjoyed!"

The ground tilted beneath Han's feet. He pushed Mr. Sing back so he could see the man's face. "What?" he cried. "What did you say about Father?"

The herbalist beamed. "We thought you were dead. Your father has been heartbroken."

Han's legs turned to jelly. He clutched Mr. Sing's jacket so he would not collapse. "Father is alive," he whispered.

"Yes!" Mr. Sing proclaimed. "And so are you!"

There, in the ashes of Chinatown, Han learned the story of Father's survival. The bullet had entered the outer lining of his stomach, skirted his vital organs, and exited out his back. After the bearded soldier had chased Han away, he left Father to pursue a looter. The young soldier put Father in the back of the wagon and transported him to the Ferry Building with the other wounded. There, he was sent by barge to a hospital in Oakland. Father remained in the hospital for five days because the wound became infected. Since then, he has been recuperating in the refugee center established by the Methodist church in Oakland.

"My wife is caring for him there," Mr. Sing said. "I have returned today to begin arranging the rebuilding process. I'm staying with a friend whose house survived."

"I must see him!" Han cried. "How can I get to Oakland?"

Mr. Sing scratched his head. "Tomorrow, can you meet me at Lafayette Park at 10:00 a.m.? The Chinese Benevolent Association will be distributing aid and discussing how to rebuild Chinatown. Someone there will help you."

Han agreed and Mr. Sing left. An electrifying energy buzzed through Han. He slipped the mahjong dice and his queue into his pocket with his other belongings. The dice clicked against the coins the crew had given him. The card with the captain's address was tucked inside the book of proverbs. The frizzled queue draped over everything.

The weight of these belongings felt just right against Han's hip. Pieces of his Chinese self and pieces of his American self, all mixed up together.

Chapter 12

May 13, 1906

The nameplate on the man's desk read George Maus, and the clerk looked so much like a rodent that Han could not help but stare. Mr. Maus's mouth turned down and his nose turned up. When his glasses slid down, instead of pushing them up with his finger, Mr. Maus wriggled his nose. This made his bushy mustache twitch. Han pressed his lips together so he would not snicker. He did not want to laugh at the person who held the Liu family's future in his hands.

"So are you here to get a new certificate of residence?" Mr. Maus's head bent over a stack of papers.

Father opened his mouth, but Han answered first. "No, my father needs a new birth certificate. His was destroyed in the fire that burned our grocery store."

The chairs Han and Father sat in were so close that their elbows touched. Han felt Father's body stiffen beside him. He prayed Father would keep silent.

As they had walked to Franklin Hall that morning, Father kept complaining that he felt like a Chinese sausage. He and Han were both wearing clothes they had received from the Chinese Benevolent Association. The donations were limited, so Han was wearing western-style clothes and Father had received a tunic one size too small.

As Father grumbled that his buttons were too tight and his sleeves too short, a plan had formed in Han's mind. He was not sure it would work, but he *was* sure that if he told Father about the idea, Father would say *absolutely not*. So, the only warning Han gave him before they entered the temporary records office was a proverb.

"Remember this," Han whispered into Father's ear. "'A wise man before a magistrate will be mute for a while.'"

Father had given him a *what-are-you-talking-about* look. The plan could flop, but when Han saw the mousey clerk, he threw caution to the wind and decided to try it.

Mr. Maus glanced up at Han. "I was asking your pa."

Han looked down at his lap, as though overcome with emotion. "I'm sorry. My father was injured during the disaster. The doctor ordered him not to speak for five more days."

Mr. Maus looked at Father.

Father looked at Han.

"You suffered an injury?" Mr. Maus asked.

For several long seconds, Father hesitated. Finally, he nodded.

The clerk's gaze took in Father's sickly color and gaunt face. Father looked like a man who had been close to death. When Han first visited Father at the refugee center in Oakland, Father's appearance had stunned him. His strong giant of a father now walked with a stoop, and his hair had turned almost completely gray.

"Father was almost killed," Han said. "He was trying to rescue things from the ruins of our store after the earthquake. A soldier thought he was looting and shot him."

Mr. Maus wriggled his nose three times in rapid succession. "I've read newspaper stories about that happening. Shocking!"

"Yes." Han lifted Father's tunic to reveal the wide bandage wrapped around Father's belly. Father shoved Han's hand away, but not before Mr. Maus saw the bandage.

"Whoa, you *are* a lucky fellow."

Father nodded, his lips pressed into a narrow line.

"But, I'm confused. How does a wound in the belly affect your ability to talk?"

Han internally smacked himself in the forehead. "Uh, well . . ." he stuttered, trying to piece together a logical story. "The soldier left Father for dead."

The best lie was one closest to the truth. Han wondered if that was a proverb. If it was not, it should be.

"The fire destroyed our family store," he continued.

Mr. Maus frowned. "How'd he escape?" He pointed at Father, but looked to Han for answers.

Han clasped his hands together. "Thankfully, another soldier came by with a wagon. He was a kindhearted man. He saw Father in the wreckage and saved him."

Father was glaring at Han, but Han just smiled. All true so far.

"But Father had inhaled a lot of smoke. Damaged in here." Han ran one hand up and down his own throat. Then he tapped his chest. "And in here too."

Mr. Maus nodded slowly. "Lucky, lucky man."

Father said nothing.

Mr. Maus tapped an index finger on his typewriter. "Better get down to business. Now you say your Father needs a new birth certificate, but you need to go to the Chinese embassy for that. I can only issue certificates for American citizens."

Han swallowed. "We are American citizens."

Mr. Maus wriggled his whiskers. "Your father too?"

"Of course. That's why we're here."

Mr. Maus frowned at Father, who did not look away. "Where was he born?"

"San Francisco," said Han.

Mr. Maus leaned over the typewriter and stared hard at Han. "What year?"

Han froze. He couldn't remember what year Father had been born or even how old he was. They had not celebrated Father's birthday last year, because Mother and Meiying had just left and neither he nor Father felt very cheerful.

Han's brain raced through the numbers. The Chinese Exclusion Act prevented Chinese people from immigrating to the United States in 1882, so Han had to make Father ng enough to have a twelve-year-old son, but old ough to have been born in the country before its doors were slammed to Asia. Did he need to add to Father's real age? Or subtract?

"Um, well, he was born in . . ."

"1860," Father whispered. It sounded like he had scraped the words out of his throat with a knife.

Mr. Maus grimaced. "Oooh, ouch. Please, do not strain your throat."

Father nodded gratefully.

Han bit back a grin. Now he remembered. Father was born in 1860 and Mother in 1861. They had come to the United States right after they got married in April of 1882, one month before the Chinese Exclusion Act became law. Father had not needed to lie.

The rest of the appointment went as smooth as butter. Father and Han walked down the steps of Franklin Hall, both carrying new birth certificates. Father was now a citizen of the United States.

The walk to Chinatown was slow and silent. Father had only returned from Oakland the day before. Han's one visit to the refugee center in Oakland had been brief. The facility was so overcrowded that Han had returned to the Presidio. Now that Father was stronger and the man with nightmares had left, Father moved into the tent with Han.

Although he was still weak, Father insisted on seeing the store site with his own eyes. They passed Portsmouth Square. Han looked away from the fresh mounds of dirt. In the days after the quake, hundreds of dead had been hastily buried in mass graves in city parks. Han was grateful Father did not wind up there.

"Why did you do that?" Father asked.

Han had been waiting for the question. "It was our chance. So I took it."

"It was an untruth," Father shot back.

"You must have heard the talk among the refugees in Oakland," Han said. "When City Hall burned, all official records were destroyed. People who are not citizens can claim they were born here and the government can't prove otherwise."

Father frowned. "An untruthful man is iron without steel."

Han groaned inwardly. Even a brush with death had not lessened Father's love of proverbs. "Do you remember what you said about filial piety keeping the universe in balance?"

A cloud passed over Father's face. "I am sorry for blaming you for waking the Earth Dragon. It takes more than one young boy's impulsive action to stir that monster."

Han shook his head. "I don't mean that. Anyway, there is no Earth Dragon. Geology caused the earthquake." When Father started to disagree, Han put his hand up. "We can argue about that later. I meant what you told me the night before the quake. You said that filial piety moves heaven and earth."

"After you cut off your queue?" Father eyed the back of Han's head with an unreadable expression. He stumbled on a piece of rubble and Han took his arm. They turned down Sacramento Street.

"There is a proverb that says"—Han waved one hand in the air, trying to remember the exact words—"something like, 'Children should serve their parents properly while they are living, bury them with proper rites when they die, and worship them afterward with proper sacrifices.'"

Father stopped and stared at Han as though he had never seen him before. "How do you know this?"

But Han was not finished. "How do you expect me to properly care for Mother when she is thousands of miles away? What if you were deported back to China, which could happen if you weren't a citizen? How could I bury you properly?"

"But how do you know these things?" Father asked again.

"I read them in that book you gave me," Han answered.

Father fell silent for a long time. Han glanced at him and saw his throat working rapidly up and down. When Father finally spoke, his voice was thick with emotion. "I thought *Proverbs* was destroyed in the fire."

Han shook his head. "It was in the basket that I took on the morning of the quake. I've had it with me the entire time."

Father gripped Han's arm tighter. "Has it guided your path?"

Han grinned. "Actually, yes."

He told Father how *Proverbs* had led him to help the grandmother and little Jun, and had given him the guts to frighten the grave robbers, barter wisdom for water at the street camp, and seize his opportunity from Captain Thorrold.

An *I-told-you-so* smile spread over Father's face.

"But," Han added quickly, "*The Adventures of Tom Sawyer* helped me too." He explained how he had fooled the soldiers into helping him free the wheelbarrow.

Father erupted in laughter. He released Han's elbow and clapped him on the back. "Maybe it's time that I read about Mr. Sawyer."

When they arrived at the store site, Father immediately turned somber. Now even the rubble, beams, and ash had vanished. Where the Liu Grocery & Dry Goods store had once stood was only a patch of earth.

Father wiped away a tear, and Han's heart ached.

"My life's work has been erased," said Father.

"Only for the moment," Han said. "The leaders of the Chinese Benevolent Association want property owners to rebuild as soon as possible. As I told you, they've hired me and lots of other boys and men from the Presidio to clean up. I'm making money, Father."

Father made a face. "We will need it."

"Miss Cameron is down here every day," Han continued. "She's rebuilding the Occidental Mission Home for Girls, and she's been pestering me to hurry and reopen the store so she can get her stock of sugared almonds."

Father shot Han a sidelong glance. "I suspect she's providing you with a steady supply of American novels too."

Han thought of the copy of *Treasure Island* under his pillow in the tent and shrugged. Somehow he did not think he and Father would argue over what books Han read anymore.

Father ran a hand over his face. "The thing is, Han, you say you're an American, and you are. But your mother and sister are in China. I'd hoped to have enough money saved up this year so we could return and I could buy a small store there to support us. But with this,"—he gestured to the empty lot—"it will take years to replenish the money

I've lost. Who knows when we'll see your mother and sister again?"

Han faced Father. "America is my home, and it's Meiying's too. And if you think about it, you and Mother have lived here longer than you lived in China. Why not make America your home?"

Father's eyes swam with tears. "How can I? My wife and my daughter are an ocean away."

"Bring them here. You can do it now."

Father's brow furrowed in confusion.

"You're a citizen," Han reminded him. "You have the right to bring your wife and your daughter to America. You already own land here. You're already an established businessman here. Your children are citizens here."

Realization dawned in Father's eyes. "I can bring them here."

"It would be quicker and cheaper than trying to save enough money to return to China and buy property there," Han said.

"A new life in a new Chinatown," Father said. He looked at the empty lot and his eyes took on a dreamy expression.

"When I attended the meeting of the Chinese Benevolent Association, the leaders talked about building a better Chinatown. They are giving out loans and grants," Han said. "Picture it, Father."

They stood side by side, each with his own vision. In Han's wakeful dream, he and Meiying walked home from school together. Han's hair was short, and he wore trousers and a button-down shirt, and Meiying wore a blue flowered dress. The cobblestone was gone, and Dupont Street was paved, broad sidewalks lining each side. A garbage wagon stopped in front of the butcher shop. It came by daily now, so the street was clean and the neighborhood smelled of incense, spices, and delicious food.

In Han's daydream, a bright-yellow building occupied the corner of the block. A red pagoda crested the top floor, and the lower floor had a roof with curled eaves. The motif of a green dragon breathing fire wound along the concrete sides. The building looked like it had sprung straight from the pages of Chinese folklore.

The top floor held a large apartment with three bedrooms. Instead of a sink and privy in the back alley, the apartment had a kitchen and bathroom with indoor plumbing.

The red lettering on the sign across the front of the building swirled and danced in both English letters and Chinese characters: Liu Grocery & Dry Goods.

In his mind, Han opened the door. The scent of jasmine tea and the sound of laughter greeted him. He took his sister's hand and drew her inside.

Han turned to see Father watching him, a gentle smile on his face.

Han tried to remember where he'd left off in his description of what the Chinese leaders were planning. "They said they want Chinatown to be a neighborhood of palaces that will look more Chinese than China."

Father chuckled. "It will be an American Chinatown." He slung one arm around Han's shoulder and ruffled his short hair. "For an American boy."

Later that night, Han sat on his cot in the tent at the Presidio, licked the tip of his pencil, and began to write.

May 13, 1906
Dear Mother and Meiying,

I have good news. Pack your bags. Before the year is up, you'll both be on a ship to America. . . .

Author's Note

This book is a work of fiction, and Han Liu is a character of my imagination. However, many of the beliefs that Han and his father hold are based on historical records. Hugh K. Liang was a Chinese American teenager living in San Francisco when the earthquake struck. Before he died in 1983, Liang wrote a partial memoir. The Chinese Historical Society of San Diego published Liang's account of the 1906 disaster in its spring 1996 newsletter. According to Liang, the Chinese believed that an earth dragon controlled the planet and caused earthquakes. Usually, the creature slept for decades, but when it woke and moved its body, the earth shook. Liang recorded that when the earthquake struck on April 18, 1906, his cousin woke him by shouting, "Dey loong jun." The Earth Dragon.

In *The Great Earthquake and Firestorms of 1906: How San Francisco Nearly Destroyed Itself*, Philip L. Fradkin discusses the Chinese belief that four bulls held up the world. He also describes how shortly after the earthquake, a steer did in fact escape from a nearby stockyard and run through Portsmouth Square.

At Chinese school, Han would probably have learned traditional Chinese values from books called the *Analects*, *Three Character Classic*, or *Di Zi Gui*. However, for the purposes of this story, I used proverbs from *A Collection of Chinese Proverbs*, published in 1875. This collection was translated and arranged by William Scarborough, a Christian missionary in China. The sayings are not a literal translation of their original Chinese meaning. Over time, the phrases became "transculturated," a process in which elements of one culture are passed on to another culture and modified along the way. But the phrases are brief and colorful, and their meaning is often mysterious. Deciphering the proverbs is important to Han's struggle with determining his own identity as a Chinese American boy.

Many of the challenges Han faces are based on historical facts. Anti-Chinese racism was very real in the late nineteenth century, which had a boom-and-bust economy. When jobs were scarce, white Americans resented Chinese immigrants who were willing to work for low pay. Local politicians fanned the flames of racism, and in 1882, Congress passed the Chinese Exclusion Act. This law banned the immigration of Chinese laborers, required people of Chinese origin to carry identification documents, and prohibited Chinese people from becoming naturalized American citizens. The law caused a decline in the number of Chinese immigrants and made it very difficult for any immigrants who had left the United States, such as Han's mother, to return.

Additionally, fires caused by the US Army did destroy Chinatown, although this was on accident. Shortly after the earthquake struck, more than fifty small fires ignited throughout San Francisco. With the water mains broken, the city did not have enough water to put out the fires. At 6:30 a.m. on April 18, the fire department sent a message to the Presidio requesting all available explosives and soldiers be sent into the city. Authorities had decided to use dynamite to explode some buildings in order to create firebreaks, or open gaps, between structures to deprive the fire of fuel.

At 5:00 p.m. that day, General Funston gave the order to blow up a drugstore that bordered Chinatown. By this time, the Army had run out of dynamite, so soldiers used gunpowder instead, which was much harder to control. When the drugstore exploded, it hurled a burning mattress across the street. The mattress ignited a house on the edge of Chinatown. Soon, the entire neighborhood was ablaze. In the story, I moved the time of the explosion to earlier in the day so that Han would not be able to return to the store to find his father.

Soldiers did have permission to shoot suspected looters. In the morning of April 18, San Francisco mayor Eugene Schmitz issued a shoot-to-kill directive to all law enforcement officers. Anyone caught looting or committing any other crime could be shot. This was done to prevent people from trying to steal from the US Mint. At the time of the fire, this building held one-third of the entire nation's gold reserves.

However, the neighborhood that was most heavily looted after the fire was Chinatown. On April 27, city authorities allowed visitors to reenter the city for the first time, and many headed for Chinatown. The *San Francisco Chronicle* reported that 150 members of the National

Guard from Oakland were among the first looters that day. On the afternoon of April 28, more than 1,000 people carried pilfered goods such as porcelain plates, teapots, and pitchers, and sold them along Market Street. More serious burglars searched for safes and vaults. While their property was being pilfered, Chinese people were not permitted to return home until April 30.

Two characters in the book are based on real people. Donaldina Cameron was the superintendent for the Occidental Mission Home for Girls, a school founded in 1874 to aid victims of human trafficking. Cameron came to teach at the school in 1895 and was named superintendent two years later. The school withstood the earthquake but was destroyed by dynamite. Cameron and all the students survived. She rebuilt the school on the same spot. The building still stands. Today, it is called Cameron House, and it serves low-income and immigrant youth and their families.

Eliza Thorrold was the first licensed female tugboat pilot on the San Francisco Bay. After her husband, Captain Charles Thorrold, died of blood poisoning in 1896, Eliza

Thorrold continued to operate the Ethel and Marion, her steam tugboat. However, the law required a licensed master aboard to transact business. Believing it was a waste of money to hire a man for a job she could do herself, Thorrold applied for and received a license. She sold the tugboat in 1900. There is no record of it being used in the rescue efforts during the 1906 fire.

Children cross the street in San Francisco's Chinatown in 1896.

Two children stand on a sidewalk in Chinatown in 1896.

After the earthquake, people in San Francisco watch as fires in the distance burn their city.

A man walks among the wreckage of the San Francisco earthquake and fire.

Map

(engraved and printed in 1885)

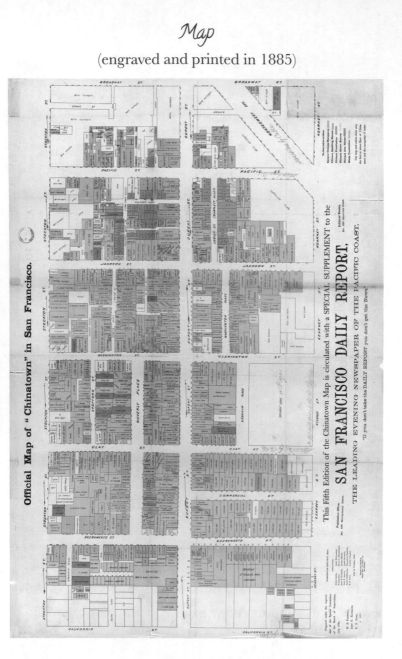

1906 Earthquake and Fire

Prior to 1906, scientists understood very little about earthquakes. The first seismographs were installed in California in 1887, and a few geologists worked to observe earthquakes' features. The 1906 earthquake was a turning point. After this disaster, the scientific study of the San Andreas Fault began.

The San Andreas Fault is a ten-mile-deep gash in the bedrock of California. It runs for 800 miles and ends north of San Francisco. Earth's crust, made up of slabs of bedrock called tectonic plates, fits together like a puzzle and can only be separated by a powerful force. That force is Earth's core, which is as hot as the surface of the sun. This heat sends pressure waves to the surface. These waves create cracks in the tectonic plates that are called fault lines. When the pressure becomes too intense, the plates slide side to side or up and down, releasing shock waves above the surface. This is an earthquake.

The 1906 earthquake struck at 5:12 a.m. The quake ruptured the northern 296 miles of the San Andreas Fault, splitting the earth at a speed of 8,300 miles per hour. It measured 8.3 on the Richter scale and lasted roughly seventy-five seconds. Several aftershocks followed. Within fifteen minutes, more than fifty fires had started around the city.

Prior to the earthquake, San Francisco Fire Chief Dennis Sullivan had spent thirteen years asking city officials to make improvements to protect the city. San Francisco did not have enough pipes to distribute water in case of a major fire. Nor did it have sufficient water pressure so hoses could reach flames in tall buildings. Sullivan wanted the firefighters trained in how to use dynamite to create firebreaks, and he asked city officials to construct pumping stations to conduct salt water from the bay into the city.

The San Francisco Board of Supervisors and Mayor Eugene Schmitz had denied all these requests. Attorney Abe Ruef was San Francisco's city boss, the man who wielded power behind the scenes through illegal means. In 1901, Ruef had schemed to get his own candidate, Eugene Schmitz, elected mayor. Both men and the members of the Board of Supervisors took bribes from anyone who wanted a license to do business in San Francisco. The improvements Chief Sullivan wanted were not going to make them richer, so the politicians refused to fund them.

Sullivan finally scheduled a meeting with a federal judge to force the city to improve fire safety. However, the meeting was scheduled for April 18, 1906—the day the earthquake struck. The quake sent Sullivan plummeting through the floor of his apartment down to the cellar. He was severely injured by the fall and died four days later. Sullivan's death left a leadership vacuum right when the city needed him most.

Both San Francisco Mayor Eugene Schmitz and Brigadier General Frederick Funston of the Presidio tried to take command during the chaos. Schmitz, concerned about maintaining order, authorized both soldiers and police to shoot looters on sight, no questions asked. After the disaster ended, the military claimed only three men were shot, but eyewitness accounts suggest the number could have been as high as 500.

The official death toll for the earthquake and fire was 498 people, a figure historians dismiss as inaccurate. A modern researcher conducted an in-depth study and concluded the actual number of dead fell between 5,000 and 10,000 people. The fire burned 520 city blocks and 28,188 buildings, leaving 250,000 people homeless.

Chinese Citizenship

The disaster had one silver lining for Chinese immigrants. Because all vital records were destroyed when City Hall was burned, Chinese immigrants could claim to be American citizens and officials could not disprove it. According to the law, any child of an American citizen is automatically born a citizen.

After the fire, a massive immigration fraud began. A Chinese immigrant with new proof of citizenship could obtain a legal document to let his or her children enter the country. Cousins, nephews, and nieces pretended to be the children of these new citizens, and many of these "paper sons" and "paper daughters" were complete strangers willing to pay a steep fee to get into the United States.

Once the US government caught on to the scheme, Chinese people trying to enter the country were detained at Angel Island in the San Francisco Bay and interrogated carefully about their "relatives." Of the 175,000 Chinese people who immigrated to the United States between 1910 and 1940, between 80 and 90 percent were paper sons and daughters.

Discriminatory citizenship and immigration laws lasted well into the twentieth century. Chinese immigrants could not become naturalized American citizens until 1943, when the Chinese Exclusion Act was repealed. Even then, a quota limited the number of people of Chinese ethnicity who could immigrate to only 105 annually. Immigration restrictions against the Chinese did not end until 1965, when the law was changed.

The Location of Chinatown

City authorities had long wanted to relocate Chinatown, and they saw the disaster as their chance to make it happen. The sixteen blocks that had been Chinatown sat between Nob Hill and the Financial District, and included some of the most valuable property in the city. Many white businesses wanted that land.

Only six days after the fire, the mayor established the Committee on the Location of Chinatown. The group did not include a single Chinese member. Members quickly voted to move the Chinese to Hunters Point, a remote piece of land six miles away from the original Chinatown. The committee presented its proposal at a meeting with representatives of Chinatown's Family Associations and a representative of the Chinese government. It soon became clear that any possibility of relocating Chinatown was doomed.

First, the Chinese government opposed such a move. The Chinese embassy had been located in the old Chinatown, and the Chinese government owned the land on which it had stood. The Chinese ambassador notified the governor of California and San Francisco officials that China would rebuild its embassy on the exact same spot as the old one.

Chinese merchants presented the second obstacle to relocating Chinatown. They threatened to leave San

Francisco altogether rather than rebuild at Hunters Point. White landlords made a lot of money from renting buildings to the Chinese, and the city received millions of dollars in tax revenue from Chinese merchants. If San Francisco's Chinese population moved to Oakland or Seattle, this money would disappear too.

Finally, Chinese people did not wait for city officials to decide to relocate them. Many people simply moved back into their burned neighborhood. With salvaged boards and bricks, they built temporary houses and shops and restarted their lives. A group of the largest and wealthiest Chinese merchants pooled their money and hired an architectural firm to design a new and improved Chinatown. The architects in this firm were white men whose only knowledge of Chinese architecture was pagodas, or multi-tiered religious temples. So, the pagoda became the trademark building of the new Chinatown, which was completed by 1908.

About the Author

Judy Dodge Cummings has written more than twenty-five books for children and teenagers. A veteran high school social studies teacher, Judy's passion is history. After teaching for twenty-six years, she earned an MFA in Creative Writing for Children from Hamline University and began to write the history she so loved to teach. She writes both fiction and nonfiction, and her goal is to write books that transport young readers back in time. Judy lives in south-central Wisconsin with her husband, three cats, and too many books to count.

About the Consultant

Dr. Lei Qin is an Assistant Adjunct Professor in Asian Studies at the University of California, Los Angeles. Her research specialty lies in modern Chinese culture, history, and politics, while her teaching focuses on modern Chinese culture, literature, and history.

About the Illustrator

Eric Freeberg has illustrated over twenty-five books for children and has created work for magazines and ad campaigns. He was a winner of the 2010 London Book Fair's Children's Illustration Competition; the 2010 Holbein Prize for Fantasy Art, International Illustration Competition, Japan Illustrators' Association; Runner-Up, 2013 SCBWI Magazine Merit Award; Honorable Mention, 2009 SCBWI Don Freeman Portfolio Competition; and 2nd Prize, 2009 Clymer Museum's Annual Illustration Invitational. He was also a winner of the Elizabeth Greenshields Foundation Award.